THE MAGICAL
PEPPERS
AND THE ISLAND OF INVENTION

First published in Great Britain by
HarperCollins Children's Books in 2012
HarperCollins Children's Books is a division of
HarperCollinsPublishers Ltd,
77-85 Fulham Palace Road, Hammersmith, London W6 8JB

The HarperCollins website address is
www.harpercollins.co.uk

1

ISBN-13 978-0-00-743002-4

Printed and bound in England by
Clays Ltd, St Ives plc

MIX
Paper from
responsible sources
FSC www.fsc.org **FSC C007454**

THE MAGICAL PEPPERS

AND THE ISLAND OF INVENTION

SIÂN PATTENDEN

Illustrated by Jess Mikhail

HarperCollins *Children's Books*

The Troupe

Uncle Potty

Mr Portobello

Monty

Esmé

Keith

Tabitha & Twinkle

Deirdre & Bernard

Stupeedo

Contents

Dr Pompkins – Totality Magic

Welcome once more to the magic world of Dr Pompkins. As I sit at my study chair with a small pot of tea and a basket of fresh pastries there is just one word I'd like to mention: *style*. Now that you have learned the basics of magic, you need to know how to augment your tricks with verve and panache – this is as necessary as your practical know-how. If you follow me through these colossal pages, dear reader, you will learn how to make every trick your own. The world is our oyster… and we are but hungry explorers on a mountain ledge of possibility…

In all totality,

Dr Pompkins

CHAPTER ONE

The Sea Spray Theatre

Boomph!

Esmé and Monty Pepper were on the beach when they heard the first explosion.

"What was that?" asked Monty, turning round.

"It came from that tiny island just out to sea," replied Esmé, who had been looking for fossils. "I wonder what could have caused it." Esmé wrinkled her brow and stood up facing the island, which looked like a palm tree pudding in a bowl of blue custard.

Boooomph!

There was *another* bang, bigger this time and closer.

"Oh, dear," said Monty.

"It's Potty!" said Esmé. "Come on, take your flippers off, Monty – we'd better go and check if he's all right."

It was springtime and the Pepper twins were spending the school break at the seaside with Potty – a professional and very tall magician with wispy, worm-like hair and one long eyebrow.

Potty had done a good job of looking after Esmé and Monty last summer. When they had arrived back from holiday, Mr and Mrs Pepper were impressed to hear how the twins had saved a local magic club and organised its new junior division. Now, Esmé and Monty's hippie parents wanted to use the springtime school break to catch a quick glimpse of the Sacred Mountain of Terry in Goa, and sing a hymn to the Indian Goddess of Soil – or something like that. So again they entrusted Potty to look after their children at the seaside while he put on his latest Sea Spray Theatre show at the end of Crab Pie Pier.

Had Mr and Mrs Pepper been given details about last summer's exploding toaster, flooded kitchen, spilt baked beans, damaged laptop, etc. then they might have thought twice about leaving their children with Potty again. But, luckily for Esmé and

13

Monty, they weren't told anything of the sort.

By the sound of explosion number two, Potty was up to his old tricks again. The twins ran towards the theatre as fast as they could.

Esmé, dressed with practicality in mind for a spring break on the British coast, was wearing a yellow mac over a sweatshirt and navy blue straight-fit trousers. Her plimsolls had plenty of grip that helped her to run across the pebbly beach without slipping. Monty, on the other hand, had dressed this morning in a Victorian blue-and-white striped bathing suit, complete with rubber ring and flippers, and his usual black velvet cape. Having been on the beach for the last two hours, Monty had picked up plenty of seaweed, which hung from his rubber ring and made him look like a cross between a sea monster and a chandelier. The curling fronds of seaweed trailed behind him as they ran up the steps to the Sea Spray Theatre.

The Sea Spray Theatre had been built on Crab Pie Pier in the 1930s. Throughout the decades it had played host to many top names: Pat Daniels, Timothy Cooper, Fay Presto. It was a great example of art deco architecture – featuring a curved facade, wooden panels around the front entrance and magnificent geometric arches along the roof. Well, it would have been a great example if the exterior had not been crumbling away – decades of salty air biting into the smooth, rendered surface, destroying the varnish on the wooden panels and bleaching the once-bright colours. The seagulls that always sat in a line along the top of the building had also added their own, rather sticky, decoration over the years.

The twins came running in through the main entrance, knocked over the spider plant by the main door and rushed into the auditorium.

"Potty, Potty!" called Monty. "Are you OK? We heard a loud noise…"

Potty stood alone on the dim, unlit stage.

He was wrapped up in a huge fishing net, struggling to get out. Underneath he wore a brand new cape, which had replaced the old tweed one because it smelt of smoked mackerel. This cape was yellow with vertical satin stripes and had the words, 'The Potty

Magician' sewn on the back. Esmé thought that it made Potty look like a particularly happy banana.

"Oh, *totality*," said Potty when he saw the Pepper twins, his huge eyebrow knotting into a frown. "I've blown the lights."

"What happened?" asked Esmé.

Potty sighed. He was not a happy banana.

"I was trying to come up with the main trick for my new show," he explained, gesticulating under the net. "I heard the sound of the waves lashing against the beach, the wind whistling over the sea and the seagulls squealing outside. I closed my eyes, trying to capture the essence of the great briney oceans thereof."

"Briney oceans thereof?" asked Monty.

"Certainly, and very cold too," replied Potty. "One minute I'm experimenting with the Flying Fish trick – the next minute the small turbot in my hand explodes and fuses the lights."

"You had a live fish in your hand?"

"It's not a *real* one," answered Potty. "It's made out of rubber." He pointed to his left. "It's over there."

"I see," said Esmé, glancing at the small fish lying on the ground.

"Then I got caught up in the net..." explained Potty. "And now I can't get out."

"We'll help," said Esmé.

"Wonderful," beamed Potty. "The fact that I had spring-loaded the fish beforehand may have added to the problem."

"Oh, dear," said Esmé, trying to disentangle Potty. She remembered the toaster incident from last summer, when Potty decided to heat up a dynamite sandwich. "We had better phone the theatre owners."

"No need," replied Potty, his long, banana-coloured limbs now almost free of the net. "The Table sisters own the place – they live down the pier in the gypsy caravan, to the left of the coconut shy."

"OK," said Esmé, moving towards the auditorium door. "You and Monty stay here and tidy things up a bit and I'll go and let them know what's happened…"

Dr Pompkins – Totality Magic

TRICK: How to Walk Through a Postcard

Friends, this is a marvellous trick, which goes back to Victorian times. Tell your chums that you can walk through a postcard.

It seems impossible, but fold a postcard lengthways, take a very sharp pair of scissors and cut like so {see fig. 1}, making a series of sideways slits.

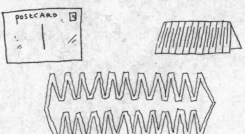

Carefully open the card and see how it expands into a ring of enormous girth. Step into it, pull it up to your middle then over your head.

———

A resounding, "Amazing!" will be the cry from your audience.

Opening Act

At the start of your show, when the curtains open and you walk out on stage or at a simple gathering, the first thing that everyone will notice is your outward appearance… Walk briskly, as soon as your name is announced – the audience will see that you mean business. Smile to acknowledge the applause and start your act immediately. Confidence is all – get in there and do it.

Your exit is just as important; take your time to smile and bow. If you have performed well, come back on stage again – but only if the audience still applauds. If they have run away, have a big think about becoming a magician. You might want to look into the role of a chartered surveyor instead.

In all totality,

Dr Pompkins

CHAPTER TWO

Teapots and Light Bulbs

Esmé walked out into the afternoon sunshine. The pier was buzzing with activity. Visitors munched from large bags of candy floss and gnawed at brittle Crab Pie rock. The radio from the coconut shy was playing loud pop music and the seagulls squawked sharply overhead. It was a splendid day, a perfect seaside morning. Apart from the strong breeze Esmé could detect from the ocean. And was that a storm cloud in the distance?

23

Esmé reached the gypsy caravan within a minute. Outside was a plyboard sign that read "Tabitha and Twinkle Table, fortune tellers to the stars – £10 for a future you'll never forget!" Underneath was pinned a signed photograph of the boxer Frank Pruno.

Esmé raised her hand to knock at the wooden door of the caravan.

"Come in, deary," came a voice, a fraction of a second before Esmé's knuckles touched the wood.

Esmé popped her head through the door. It was completely dark inside. "H-hello?" she stuttered. "I'm Esmé Pepper, the Potty Magician's niece."

"We know," said a voice from the void. There was a fumbling sound and a bare light bulb flickered on. Two smiling ladies were at once visible, sitting around a square table. The Table sisters must have been in their eighties but their eyes shone like baubles on a Christmas tree.

"I'm Tabitha Table, and this is my sister, Twinkle." Tabitha thrust out a large hand in greeting and smiled, revealing slightly fewer teeth than Esmé had expected. She wore a dusty-pink cardigan, a white shirt and green nylon trousers.

Twinkle Table seemed smaller – and shyer – than her sister. She had a kind expression on her face, and fine features, with a distinctive beauty spot painted on to her left cheek. She wore a purple dress with tassels falling from the hem, and long

25

lengths of russet-coloured chiffon hanging loosely around her shoulders and over her head. From her ears hung large dangly earrings shaped like feathers, which made a soft sound whenever she moved.

The small table in front of them was filled with objects. Two pairs of binoculars, a china teacup and a gleaming crystal ball. From the ceiling of the caravan hung various items – an old gas lamp, a set of wood chimes, a large metal teapot, tea cups, a bundle of small white crystals and what looked like a long jawbone filled with three rows of pointy teeth.

"Mandible of the trout," explained Tabitha matter-of-factly. Esmé noticed her fingers were adorned with enormous mystical-looking jewellery: a large ring in the shape of a frog, one that looked like a crown and another a skull. They clicked sharply together as Tabitha pointed to the jawbone. "Brings us good luck and you can also use it as a cake ingredient."

Esmé thought that sounded rather horrible, but chose not to say anything.

"Do sit down," said Twinkle softly to Esmé. "Would you like us to read your destiny?" she asked, trying to reach the teapot hanging from the ceiling. "The tea leaves perhaps?"

Tabitha took one look at her sister struggling and grabbed the object herself with her well-ornamented hands.

"I'm pretty sure we should be talking about practical matters, like mending the

theatre lights," Tabitha said.

Esmé blinked. *How does Tabitha know? Maybe I said something when I came in…*

Tabitha eyed Esmé's practical clothes. Esmé's cheeks began to go red – she felt out of place in the caravan with all its trinkets and wonder.

Meanwhile Twinkle fiddled with the chiffon on her head, producing a teaspoon from one of its many folds. Once her sister had finished adding tea leaves and water from the freshly boiled kettle to the pot, Twinkle stirred the contents slowly and thoughtfully with her spoon.

Tabitha brought out a packet of sweets from her pocket and offered one to Esmé. "Werther's Original?" she asked.

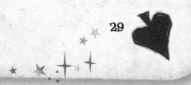

"No, thank you," said Esmé, politely.

"Aha! I can see that you are a very sensible young lady," said Tabitha. "You worry that if you take a sweet you will ruin your teeth. You don't sit down in a stranger's home until you are asked. *Hmm...* I can also tell that you do a good job looking after your twin brother and your beloved uncle."

"Tabitha, don't start yet – I haven't even spoken to the tea leaves," said Twinkle, who was still messing about with the teapot and the spoon.

"Twinkle, you know that if I am inspired I like to do my personality readings as quickly as possible," replied Tabitha, breathing in deeply, jewellery still clinking. "I can see that Esmé Pepper is a logical person and good at problem solving. I would even go so far as to say that she has a talent for it, and in the future she would make a great scientist or indeed a super sleuth."

Esmé was taken aback – and secretly impressed. Tabitha gave her a big, not-so-toothy grin.

"I'm ready now," said Twinkle Table as she concentrated hard on pouring the remnants inside the teapot into the cup in front of her. She swirled the cup in a clockwise direction and peered in. Esmé watched as Twinkle closed her eyes and wrinkled her nose. "I see a long, happy life ahead of you. I also see a small notebook and a sharpened pencil that you carry with you at all times."

Esmé flushed again – this was true.

Twinkle went silent and, teacup still in hand, her head dropped to one side and her mouth fell open. She made a small gurgling sound.

Esmé stared at Twinkle, fascinated. She had never seen anything like this before – was there something wrong?

"Is Twinkle all right?" Esmé asked Tabitha.

"She's fine," came Tabitha's reply. "Just a swoon. It's part of the reading, part of the fun."

Twinkle started murmuring. "Ah, I see a vision. An illumination, a fire in a fish tank. Yes, that's it – flames, rising high, engorging everything in their wake. Trouble, Esmé, trouble. You must be on guard at all times."

Twinkle abruptly opened her eyes. "There

was also something about 'Thai summer rolls', but I couldn't make sense of that."

Esmé was startled, but as if nothing had happened, Twinkle put the teacup down on the table and shook Esmé's hand.

"Thank you," said Twinkle, eyes shining bright. "That was a very intense reading."

"Now that's enough of the mystical stuff," remarked Tabitha. "Let's get on with fixing those theatre lights."

"We'd better phone Keith," said Twinkle, slipping into the back to make the call.

"Keith is our fix-it man," explained Tabitha. "He's very talented. He can fix or make just about anything – lights, fuses, entire air-conditioning systems that also emit the smell of patchouli oil. He built us

33

this caravan out of two hundred empty cola cans, half a canoe and some cement."

"Keith's on his way to the theatre," said Twinkle, replacing the receiver. "Let's head over and meet him there."

They all left the caravan into the sunshine outside and the three of them walked arm in arm up the pier, passing posters for Potty's show along the way.

"Our last magic show," said Tabitha, with a broad sigh.

"Why 'last'?" asked Esmé.

"Well, the truth is, we may not be in charge of the Sea Spray Theatre much longer," Twinkle told Esmé. "A local businessman named Mr Portobello is interested in buying it from us. We are relying on him to make a good offer."

"You're selling the theatre?"

"Yes," said Twinkle. Esmé noticed she was wearing tiny satin shoes with pointed toes. "We've been running the theatre for thirty years – but it's a sideline, really, to our more spiritual calling."

"If Mr Portobello offers us a healthy sum," said Tabitha brightly, "then we can not only concentrate on the psychic readings but there's a lovely bungalow on Tide Street that we would very much like to move into – more space, more light, more *resonance*. The spirits are getting sick of the caravan, there's not enough room for them. They keep bumping into each other."

Esmé smiled. She had never met anyone

who believed in spirits before, apart from Monty's dabbling in what he called 'vibrations'. She was beginning to like the Table sisters very much.

"We tried to sell the Sea Spray last year but Mr Portobello made us such a low offer we had to pull out of the deal," confided Twinkle. "It was after the famous magician Gary Meringue had been due to perform. People were queuing all the way along the pier to get a ticket..."

"Only he dropped out at the last minute," revealed Tabitha. "He simply disappeared. Whatever happened we will probably never know. We tried the spirits but they couldn't tell us either."

Esmé and the Table sisters arrived at the

theatre, walking through the front door in turn. "This is why we need Potty to *wow* the audience and *wow* Mr Portobello," Tabitha confirmed as she stopped to examine the spider plant. "The soil is a bit dry," she said, then turned to Esmé. "The offer we get rests on Potty's success."

"We will do our very best," said Esmé. "I'm sure that Potty will perform the show of a lifetime. If he can just manage to avoid getting caught up in his fishing net and his props exploding."

"He must," said Tabitha, with a serious look.

Esmé and the Table sisters entered the auditorium.

On stage Uncle Potty stood on a ladder with

Monty on his shoulders, arms outstretched. The ladder wobbled first left, then right. It wobbled forward, then back.

"*Oooph!*" said Monty.

"What are you two doing?" Esmé called out. "Be careful! You'll fall."

"We thought we'd have a look at the light fitting," shouted Potty, now extending a long leg outward to balance them both on the wobbling ladder.

"Please, come down now," urged Esmé. "There won't *be* a show if you're both in hospital."

"*Woooooargh!*"

Potty and Monty wobbled on the ladder for the last time and fell in a heap on the floor.

"*Oooofph!*" exclaimed Monty. Esmé helped Potty up.

"Are you all right?" she asked.

Potty rubbed his shin. "I think so. My new cape is slightly padded, so it softened the fall."

"I'm fine too," replied Monty who was sitting in a heap on the floor with the seaweed-strewn rubber ring still round his waist.

"Oh, dear," said Twinkle, gazing with concern at the magician and his assistant on whom all their hopes were riding.

"Hm," said Tabitha, looking first at them and then at the lights. "I hope Keith can fix this."

"I have a strong feeling that he will appear

shortly," said Twinkle, her nose twitching. "I am certain I can sense his aura, almost around the corner. Ooh, I feel a little faint."

She raised a hand to her forehead. Esmé recognised the glazed look in Twinkle's eyes from her swoon in the gypsy caravan.

"A chair!" squeaked Twinkle. Esmé ran to get one from backstage.

As Twinkle sat down, she closed her eyes and murmured softly, "Keith Chalk, the spirits tell me that you are near…" Her raised hand quivered a little, then with a thud fell on to her lap.

Tabitha opened up her skull ring and read the time from the miniature watch face inside. "Well, you did just call him."

A split second later Keith Chalk appeared

through the main door.

"Keith is here, everyone," shouted Twinkle.
"I knew it."

An excerpt from

Dr Pompkins – Totality Magic

TRICK: The Vanishing Stamp

A little close-up magic. Start by exclaiming that you can make the Queen disappear! Of course, by that you mean the Queen's head on a stamp, not the actual Queen…

Place a stamp on a table and a glass tumbler on top of it. Pour water into the glass just over halfway and place a saucer over the glass.

By the miracle of refraction, there is absolutely no way that the stamp can be seen through the glass tumbler.

———

This is so effective because it is so simple.

Stage Lighting

It's a good idea to use spotlights if you are performing on stage, but remember that strong lighting can change the appearance of things. Take care with shiny metal apparatus and glossy paint – it may reflect the light and make it difficult to see properly, even with just a desk lamp.

Stage lighting can also affect the way you will look, as it drains the colour from your face. You will look like a ghost unless you wear theatrical make-up. Ask your drama teacher or a nice lady how to use it. Mrs Dr Pompkins does my make-up every time and I look healthy and flushed 24/7.

In all totality,

Dr Pompkins

CHAPTER THREE

Keith Chalk

Potty brushed himself down as Keith walked on to the stage.

"You must be Mr Chalk," he said, holding out a long arm in greeting. "Pleased to meet you."

"Yes, I'm the fix-it man," replied Keith, surveying Monty, the fish and the fallen ladder. "Anything you need fixing, just ask me. Looks like you might want help already…"

Keith Chalk had brown curly hair, thick eyebrows and a straight nose. He wore paint-splattered overalls with pockets full of small spanners and wrenches. He held out a large hand and smiled as he was introduced to the Pepper twins.

"The first thing is that there's a small issue with the light bulbs," Tabitha told him.

Keith looked up at the lighting rig and scratched his head.

"No problem," he said, good-naturedly. "I can get this row of lights changed, but is this something that happened during rehearsal? And in which case, is it likely to happen again?"

Potty nodded. "Yes, maybe."

"If so, we could always try and cover the bulbs in thin sheets of heatproof plastic," said

45

Keith, enthusiastic about problem solving. "That should deal with the real issue."

"That's a great idea," said Potty.

"I love to think of the bigger picture," said Keith. "You're a magician then?"

"How did you guess?"

"The back of your cape has the words 'The Potty Magician' stitched into it."

Potty scratched his chin and looked with intrigue at Keith.

"I wonder if you have any thoughts on spring-loaded objects?" asked Potty.

"Always tricky. They can shoot off and end up anywhere, which can cause problems with your audience – *and* health and safety. You should really be looking at having more control."

Potty was impressed. Keith seemed to have something that Potty lacked – a practical take on adventurous ideas.

"Are you a fan of magic?" asked Potty.

"Oh, yes," said Keith. "I love the skill, the showmanship. I like to work out how the magicians do each trick – it takes a lot of technical skill to make sure everything comes to life."

Potty nodded enthusiastically in agreement.

"I've seen Pat Daniels perform live six times," continued Keith. "I even managed to catch Trev and Peller once – they did that incredible trick which made it look like Trev was covered in a million dollars' worth of banknotes and then was run over by an eighteen-wheel truck. For a start, the notes themselves can't have been real…"

"But I heard that they were," said Potty. "The money was passed around the audience beforehand…"

"They must have been switched at some point," said Keith.

"It is possible…" mused Potty.

Esmé watched Potty and Keith talk with interest – they seemed to be getting on splendidly.

"Then of course there's the truck," continued Keith eagerly, "which must have had at least one fake wheel, so that when it went over him—"

"…he wasn't injured! Of course," shouted Potty, finishing Keith's sentence. "And maybe the truck was weighted to one side, so as not to hurt poor Trev."

"That's it," said Keith. "You're a—"

"…genius!" finished Potty – and they both laughed.

At once, Esmé realised that Potty's act, as great as it was, had been missing something – a person who could make Potty's ambitions a reality. She was sure that Keith Chalk was this person.

"Uncle Potty," said Esmé, tugging on his cape. "Why doesn't Keith help you with this performance? He can make your tricks a hundred times…" Esmé was trying very hard not to say 'less prone to disaster', "…more workable. I read a book which said that many of the top magicians secretly employ inventors to make their act the most

sensational – and completely unique."

Keith looked at Esmé. "But I'm just a fix-it man."

"I think Esmé's right," cried Potty. "You love magic, you try and work out how the tricks are done... and you seem to have the technical know-how to help create some incredible, never-before-seen tricks."

"Well, I do like to tinker with electricals and gadgets," said Keith. "I've even made a few inventions of my own recently..."

"Do say you'll help us," said Esmé.

There was a long, tense pause as Keith looked lost in thought.

"Why not," he said at last. "It would be an honour."

Potty and Keith shook hands; both were

grinning widely.

Suddenly Twinkle started to swoon again. "It's terribly hot in here," she said.

"Oh, gracious, not again," said Tabitha.

"I just feel a little…" Twinkle fanned her face with her hand as she slumped back into her chair. "Ooh, the spirits!" Twinkle squeaked as she wrinkled her nose.

"Oh, deary me, not *another* premonition?" Tabitha was concerned. "You've only just finished your last one…"

"I can't help it," murmured Twinkle. "These apparitions just arrive… Might be important."

Twinkle's head drooped to one side then the other. It looked as if she was watching a very slow game of tennis.

"*Hurghmumble,*" said Twinkle. "*Flurghle-hoi...*"

"Anything bubbling up from the spirit world?" Tabitha asked her sister.

Esmé watched in wonder as Twinkle was visited – yet again – by some sort of mystical presence. Esmé wondered what she might see this time.

"I've got it." Twinkle's eyes opened and she shot up in her chair. "It's a shark in a suit, and it's coming to get us."

"A shark in a suit?" asked Tabitha. "Sharks don't wear clothes."

"Oh, but this one does..." Twinkle Table said, and shivered.

Just at that moment, a man entered the auditorium.

An excerpt from

Dr Pompkins – Totality Magic

TRICK: Remove an Ice Cube with a Piece of String

Compatriots and cavaliers, place before you a glass full of water and one ice cube. Give each of your friends a piece of string – medium length – and ask them to remove the ice cube with it.

Watch as they will try to lasso the cube out – to no avail. Once they have given up, take the string, soak it in the water then double it into a loop at the centre.

Rest this loop on top of the ice cube, pour some magic dust over both of them (the magic dust is actually *salt*, but your audience need not know this) and you will be able to lift the ice cube, which will have become frozen to the loop. The ice melts as you pour the salt on it, and refreezes when you stop.

Now that *is* magic. Oh, no, it's not – it's science.

Magic Hands

An audience is always watching a magician's hands – they are the tools of his trade – so it is very important to keep them looking good and working well.

Finger exercises:

The best way to improve your flexibility and coordination is by doing regular finger exercises like the ones described below:

Close your fingers very tightly into your palms, then open them one by one, starting with the forefinger. Then try opening alternate fingers – second finger, little finger, forefinger, third finger and so on {see fig. 1}.

①

Hold your hand up straight and separate your fingers as illustrated. Now change positions as quickly as you can {see fig. 2}.

②

Touch the tip of your little finger with the tip of your forefinger – first at the back, then quickly at the front {see fig. 3}.

③

In all totality,

Dr Pompkins

CHAPTER FOUR

Incomprehensible

"**D**o my eyes deceive me or am I getting a sneak preview of the performance?" said the man. He had in his hand a poster for Potty's magic show.

The assembled crew turned towards the darkness.

"You sneaky little ladies," the man said, wagging a finger at the Table sisters. "You didn't tell me you were planning another magic show. How wonderful!" He smiled round at everyone, although Esmé couldn't help but notice that his smile looked a little forced. *More like a grimace*, she thought to herself.

"And you must be the Potty Magician…"

"Yes, that's me," said Potty, walking forwards, squinting into the shadowy auditorium.

The man walked up to the stage and shook Potty's hand, then waved uncomfortably at Esmé and Monty. He was not used to children.

Twinkle and Tabitha rushed up to greet him.

"How nice to see you, Mr Portobello," said Tabitha, trying not to flinch as he kissed her cheek, then Twinkle's.

"Tea?" asked Twinkle.

"No, thanks, Twinks," said Mr Portobello, wiping his mouth with his sleeve.

So this is the man who wanted to buy the Sea Spray, thought Esmé.

Mr Portobello had greased-back hair and wore a shiny suit that was clearly one size too small for him. Esmé wondered what it was about him that made her feel uncomfortable, but she couldn't quite put her finger on it. But the man was, for the Table sisters, all important, so Esmé kept smiling and decided to be as charming as she could.

"Potty's act is going to be fantastic, Mr Portobello," Esmé said.

"Please, call me Ronnie," oozed Mr Portobello.

"Keith's been helping us out too and we've come up with some great ideas," Esmé continued.

"*Keith*… hmm, interesting," Mr Portobello mused, stroking his chin while staring hard at Keith. He turned to Esmé. "And are you his delightful young assistant?"

"No, *I* am, Mr Portobello," said Monty, a little annoyed.

"Wonderful!" replied the businessman, looking him up and down. "Nice swimming costume."

Mr Portobello walked up to the ladder and leant heavily upon it with a shiny elbow. "I love a magic show," he said. "I've seen all the greats – Mark Daniels, Terry Cooper, Ray Preston. Love 'em all. And I can see you're doing something really special here, in the great tradition of... um..."

"Houdini? Ali Bongo? Dante the Magician – *Sim Sala Bim?*" asked Potty.

"Bless you! *Ha ha ha!*" replied Mr Portobello, laughing loudly at his own joke. "Anyway, you're doing a great job, kids. I know that this show is going to be incomprehensible!"

Esmé wondered if he had meant to say 'incredible'. Looking around, everyone else was still smiling at Mr Portobello, each with a slightly glazed look in their eyes.

"And if the show is any good," boomed the businessman, "I'm going to buy this theatre for lots of money, renovate it and turn it into a fantastic venue that the Queen and Pete Middleton can enjoy."

"We're so glad you're behind the show," said Twinkle, simpering slightly. Esmé could tell how desperate she was to sell the theatre.

"Oh, I am," oozed Mr Portobello. "And now Keith has workshop space over at Crab Pie Island, where I live. He can see to your props there, when things are not exploding..."

"That was just a minor glitch, Mr Portobello," Keith reassured him. "I was having problems with the pincer... it's all sorted now."

Esmé realised that must have been the first explosion they had heard this morning.

"Good, good," said Mr Portobello. "And I simply *insist* you use the space there to construct your gadgets for Potty. It's the least I can do. That way I can keep an eye… I mean, help you," said Mr Portobello, correcting himself quickly.

But Esmé had heard the slip up, and didn't like the sound of it. *Why does Mr Portobello want to keep an eye on Keith?* she wondered.

Potty, however, seemed completely oblivious to the comment. "What a wonderful setting it must be, Keith," he said. "Your workshop must be an idyll in an otherwise crazy world. To turn your dreams into reality… To create and create and create!"

"You'll have to visit some day," said Mr Portobello. "See my collection of luxury boats."

"Yes, please," said Monty, who had caught some of Potty's enthusiasm.

"And of course," added Mr Portobello, "you can see some of Keith's *incomprehensible* creations."

Just then a mobile phone rang.

"Ah, David," shouted Mr Portobello into his device. "Yes. Yes, I've heard. Oh, straight away. Hm. All right, see you in a minute." He put the phone back in his pocket and sighed.

"Right, I must be off," he announced abruptly. "I have a meeting with my accountant. See you all soon."

And with that, Mr Portobello picked up his briefcase and walked with short, bold strides out of the venue.

Dr Pompkins – Totality Magic

TRICK: Torn Paper

Take a piece of A4 paper and cut it in half
lengthways.

Now make two small tears or cuts in it {see fig. 1}.
Challenge a close chum or relative to take hold of the
paper at each end and tear the strip into three
pieces.

Of course, my friend, this seems easy enough but
whoever pulls the paper will find that only one side will
tear.

Incredible dismay could follow; be ready to dispense
advice and guidance.

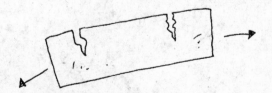

Your Notebook

You have no doubt started amassing a good quantity of tricks and ideas. You need a home for all of these and this must be a notebook. I use an Oddlerian Giltée Deluxe book, which is covered in a fine film of gold leaf and platinum strands – it has the words 'Pompkins Forever' embossed on every page. It did, however, cost £1,200 so you may want to go for something a little cheaper. It is useful at this stage in your career to write down your timings, what props you need and any special patter for each trick so you can map your act thoroughly. A lockable notebook can be good so prying magicians cannot peek at it. And maybe keep it in a top security storage building in Vienna.

In all totality,

Dr Pompkins

CHAPTER FIVE

Sir Stuart Crisps' Aquarium

As soon as Mr Portobello had left, Tabitha, Monty and Potty all started talking about him enthusiastically.

"What a nice man," said Tabitha.

"A fine chap," said Potty. "And so interested in the show."

"I can't wait to see his yachts," added Monty.

However, Esmé saw that Twinkle seemed

to be less keen than the others.

"He called me 'Twinks'," she murmured. "And I'm not sure that I feel OK about that."

"It doesn't matter what he calls you," Tabitha explained. "We need to sell the theatre and he's the only man in the area who's made an offer in the last fifteen years."

"I still have a funny feeling about it…" murmured Twinkle. "*Twinks* indeed…"

"Come along," said Tabitha, lightly tugging her sister's arm as they walked out of the theatre in a huddle. "I'll show you the figures in the caravan. We need Mr Portobello's offer sooner rather than later if we're to get that little bungalow on Tide Street…"

With the Table sisters now gone, the team

was at last left alone to concentrate on the matter in hand: the show.

"Now, we haven't quite worked out the full trick." Potty's hair wavered with extra intensity – he was thinking hard. "I'm still wondering about the aquatic theme."

"What about an enormous magic turtle leaping out of an ice cream van, Potty?" Monty asked. "Then it could turn into a hippo."

"Hmm… *not quite right.*"

"Something smaller perhaps… Terrapins jumping out of a yoghurt pot?"

"Hmm, let's start from the beginning…" replied the Potty Magician. "Elements of the ocean and the seaside are good, yes, but I want to stage something spectacular. I want the trick to be dangerous and exciting. I want it to look as if I'm in mortal danger." Potty paused. "Keith, we should try to invent some sort of device inside which I am imprisoned."

"OK… but keeping the watery theme?"

"Yes," said Potty. "Any ideas, technically speaking?"

Keith thought for a moment. "Have any of you been to the aquarium next door? If we're going take inspiration from the oceans, that's the place to go."

"Excellent," said Potty. "It might just do the trick."

And so the four intrepid researchers walked out of the theatre, along the pier and down a large flight of stone steps that led to the aquarium. The outside of the building –

similarly to the Sea Spray – had been buffeted by the salty winds of the coast for years. Paint was peeling and the once-white facade was a greeny-grey colour.

Some fading fibreglass animals were fixed on the roof of the aquarium: a large dolphin, a penguin, two crabs and a starfish. Accompanying them was a life-size model of the aquarium's founder, Sir Stuart Crisps, a Scottish diver famed for discovering a new species of coral.

Walking in, the first thing they saw were the small transparent jellyfish, which swam upward and downward in the tank as if they were in a celestial lift.

Next were the manta rays, which dipped and dived in a low pool – the aquarium

invited visitors to waggle their fingers in the water to see if the fish would come to the surface. Monty found this a great distraction and Esmé had to drag him over to the glass walk-through tunnel. Above them, graceful varieties of sea creatures glided slowly in the water – exotic squid, sullen catfish, tiny crabs and a large school of electric eels.

"The eels remind me of my houseboat years," said Uncle Potty wistfully. "I used to try and catch them but they were far too slippery."

"Were you a magician then?" asked Keith.

"Almost," replied Potty. "I was moored on a canal near Wembley. The water was calm and the weather always clement. I had a small beetle named Shep whom I fed and nurtured for a month. We talked, we shared – but eventually Shep left for pastures new and I was lonely again. I needed a hobby. I picked up a book of card tricks from the local bookshop and started to practise – it was then that I decided to become a magician. I joined the International Magic Guys – known also as the IMG – perfected more and more tricks and was never lonely again."

Keith moved them forward. "They have everyday goldfish here too," he said.

"This reminds me of the goldfish bowl trick – do you know it?" Potty asked Keith.

"Ah, the one made famous by Ching Ling Foo? Of course, it's one of the world's best tricks," replied Keith, knowledgeably. "But it's been copied a million times before…"

Potty stayed silent for a few moments, deep in thought.

"Has it been done on a *large* scale before?"

"Not that I know of," replied Keith.

"Well, that's it!" shouted Potty, leaping into the air, his yellow cape billowing in the slightly damp air of the aquarium. "I will update the trick using a *giant* fishbowl! It will be like nothing ever seen before. Keith, can you build me a tank? One big enough to stand in?"

Keith paused to think about the practicalities. "Yes, with a bit of patience it could be done."

"Perfect," said Potty, hopping on the spot. "But I need to add the element of danger... *Hmm...* I could be locked in! Can we do that too?"

"Of course, if we put a lock on it and make it appear that you can't escape – the audience will be on the edge of their seats. Naturally, you will be able to open the lid from the inside."

"If I am completely submerged in water the audience will be thrilled," said Potty, happy to have found his inspiration.

"Now, for an extra element of danger..."

"Piranhas?" suggested Monty. "Exploding from a sombrero?"

"Fire..." mused Potty, barely able to contain his ideas. "The opposite of water. Sensational..." Potty drummed his long fingers against his cheek.

"Aha! The top of the tank catches fire! Now, that *would* be something quite unforgettable.

Danger on two levels."

"A fire in a fish tank!" blurted Esmé. "That's exactly what Twinkle Table predicted."

"Did she really?" asked Keith, intrigued.

"Wow," said Monty. "She's spot on."

"It must be a good omen," announced Potty, full of vim.

"If it's done right it will be astounding," said Keith, who took out a notebook from his back pocket and jotted some ideas down. "How long have we got until the show?"

"Next Saturday – a week today," answered Potty.

"I'll go back to the island tonight and start building… Shall we meet back at the theatre on Thursday morning?"

"Splendid," remarked Potty. "Monty and

I shall work on the script, and we also have to think about costumes… I may need a waterproof cape."

Esmé saw how everyone's spirits had been lifted. Monty, for one, looked deliriously happy.

"Potty, this is the sort of thing you could get knighted for," he said, gazing up at the magician with awe.

"Now, now, let's not get carried away," answered Potty. "We must start rehearsals, and pronto!"

An excerpt from

Dr Pompkins – Totality Magic

TRICK: The World Famous Shirt Trick

You may have watched the magic lantern – the old television box – and seen the most classic 'Shirt Trick' executed with style and grace by a top magician.

The act makes the impossible possible – to look as if a gentleman's shirt can be ripped off under his suit jacket by all the mighty powers of magic.

In reality, you have agreed with the gentleman beforehand that he will tie his shirt by the cuffs and neck only {see fig. 1} – the jacket goes on afterwards.

When in front of your audience, you introduce your chap, announce you will remove his shirt, then remove the tie and release his cuff and neck buttons just before you whip off his shirt. The jacket remains.

It is simply *incredibaba*.

Travel

At some point you will be required to travel to a local fayre when your act starts gathering interest. The legendary Timothy Cooper used to travel with trunks full of tricks – much more than he would ever use at one show – just in case he needed them. Buy a good wheeled suitcase and stuff it with tricks and props. That way you will never be caught short. Also handy if you are an escapologist as you can also use it as a trunk from which to escape. Or if you need to go on holiday.

In all totality,

Dr Pompkins

CHAPTER SIX

Giant Goldfish Bowl

As the day of the big show drew near, Esmé and Monty became more and more excited. Potty worked hard on each element of the performance – how he would walk on stage, what he would wear, what he would say and where the giant fish tank would be placed for the duration of the show. Furthermore, Uncle Potty had started to time everything to the last milli-second. But after four days, he seemed to be coming to a natural halt.

"What we really need now is the tank," Potty announced on Thursday morning, just as he had completed sewing his new cape. It was made from blue satin and had fish silhouettes stitched on to it. "And we should finalise the lighting. I wonder how Keith is getting on."

"He said he'd be here today," said Esmé, putting down the bag of blue satin remnants she had been gathering from the floor. "Shall we go outside and see if we can spot him?"

In eager anticipation, Esmé and Monty stood at the end of the pier, waiting for the first glimpse of a boat arriving from Crab Pie Island. There was a strong wind blowing from the sea – the rumblings of the grumblings of stormy weather – and clouds seemed to be

gathering on the horizon, as if they too were coming to see the show.

Twenty minutes later a speck appeared on the horizon. Slowly it got closer and soon the Peppers could see a large fish tank, supported by ropes, on a rickety wooden boat. Keith caught a glimpse of the trio and waved. As he approached he mouthed something none of the three could make out, then grabbed something from his pocket and lit the top of the tank with it.

At once, a row of bright flames shone from the boat. Controlled and perfectly timed, the flames turned from red, to blue, to a bright, bright green.

"My goodness, I think he's done it!" exclaimed Potty to the Pepper twins. "Fire in a fish tank, fire upon the oceans."

It was a sight that Esmé vowed she would never forget. "It's fantastic," she said. "A feast for the eyes *and* a feat of engineering."

As the boat reached the mooring point at the end of the pier, Monty and Esmé ran down the stone steps to congratulate Keith.

"Anchors aweigh!" shouted Monty.

Esmé had to correct her brother. "What you mean is 'drop anchor'," she said. Keith, however, was preoccupied as he looked around the boat for something.

"What are you missing?" asked Esmé.

"The mooring rope!" Keith shouted up at the twins. "It's disappeared… Curses. I'm going to need some help docking this boat."

"What can we do?" called Esmé as Keith

frantically continued his search for the missing rope.

"Keith, I'll throw you my cape!" yelled Monty. He whipped the collar from his neck and reached out to Keith, but just then a particularly strong wind whipped up and swept a bewildered Keith and the fish tank right past the pier.

"Rats," said Monty. "What shall we do?"

"Monty, do you still have that extendable wand?" asked Esmé.

"Yes, it's somewhere…" said Monty, who fumbled in his sleeve, brought out the wand and elongated it to its full length. Monty leaned over and tried to hand the wand to Keith, who struggled to reach it. As the waves rose and fell, the little boat tipped from one side to the other, but at last a helpful gust of wind managed to draw a struggling Keith Chalk closer to Monty.

Keith grabbed at the wand – missed – then tried again. At last he held it tight and Monty managed to pull him in while Esmé used some string from her pocket to tie the boat to the mooring. Once steady, the Pepper twins and Keith breathed a big sigh of relief.

"That was a close one," said Keith, wiping his brow. "I wonder what happened to the mooring rope? Oh, well, no harm done. Let's carry this stuff into the theatre."

I wonder indeed, thought Esmé, remembering what Mr Portobello had said about keeping an eye on Keith. However, Esmé decided

89

to keep her thoughts to herself, for now at least.

The giant fishbowl was made out of strong plastic and had a metal lid. Keith said it had taken four days and three nights to construct it.

"The lid contains a lock which, if an audience member is to be invited on stage to test it, will seem unbreakable," Keith explained with pride. "Therefore, anyone locked inside the tank will appear to be in great peril. However, there is a secret catch, which you, Potty, will be able to unlock from inside."

"So I get inside the tank after it has been thoroughly inspected, the stage curtains close for three or four seconds, then they will open to reveal that the tank is empty. Splendid! We must test it immediately." Potty was impatient to start.

Keith suggested running a hose from the tap backstage – with Esmé holding the nozzle and Monty controlling the flow of water. The twins set it up right away.

"Ready!" called Monty when he was by the taps.

"Great, now, Monty, turn on the tap, and Esmé, please fill the bowl with water. Right to the top."

"I need to be lowered into the tank somehow," said Potty.

"No problem, I shall set up a harness and a hoist," replied Keith.

"Superb," said Potty. "You certainly are a

hard worker, Keith."

Together, Esmé and Monty managed to fill the bowl quickly while Keith prepared the harness.

"Watch out, coming down!" he yelled as a seat made out of rope descended from above the stage.

"It's completely safe," explained Keith. "Climb in, Potty, then I'll lift you up over the tank and dunk you in. Then as soon as the curtains close, you just open the lid from the inside using the secret latch," Keith told Potty, "and haul yourself out. There's an invisible step made out of transparent plastic so you can get out easily."

Potty nodded seriously, and the rehearsal began.

First, Potty spoke a few pre-rehearsed lines. He introduced the tank – "I present to you the Giant Goldfish Disappearing Bowl," – and made a joke about fish fingers, which Monty in particular enjoyed. Waving his arms Potty then announced: "I command a fire in a fish tank."

At once, four bright flames in different colours shot out of the top of the tank – helped by Keith backstage with a remote control device.

Next, Potty took off his blue satin cape and offered it to his assistant, Monty, who placed it over his arm. The harness descended. Potty grabbed it and got in.

Keith was right, the harness was strong. Standing in the wings, Keith started to hoist

Potty upwards. "Esmé!" he called. "Can you come and help me with the levers?"

Esmé smiled – she *was* rather good at working levers and pulleys – and ran over.

"Pull the switch there and Potty will start to hover over the tank," said Keith, gleefully. "Everything is running to plan." Potty swung over the tank and was gently lowered into the water. Esmé took great care in lowering him into the water. Once inside, Potty used the built-in step to reach the lid and lock it shut. Potty had shown Monty how to walk to the front of the stage and show off the key to the audience, after which Monty would pretend – using a classic technique known as 'misdirection' – to swallow the key. Esmé was impressed.

Keith pulled the curtains closed from the side of the stage and they all waited in tense excitement.

Potty, now completely submerged in the water, tried to unlock the lid – but nothing happened.

"*Buffurgle!*" Esmé heard him mumble in the water.

Monty ran to the tank and tapped it hard. "Open the lock, Uncle Potty!"

Potty tried again but it was clear the lock had stuck.

"Quick!" Esmé shouted to Keith. "The lid won't open. Do something!"

Keith ran over and fiddled with the lock. "The key, Monty! The key."

Inside the tank Potty's face turned from

red to purple. His hands started glowing silvery white as they tried again – and failed again – to release the catch.

"Potty!" cried Esmé, fearing the worst.

Potty scrabbled at the lid then started banging the side of the tank.

"It's no use," shouted Keith. "The walls are made of reinforced plastic."

Potty's eyes were now wide and his face was a greeny sort of mauve. He stared out at everyone with the vacant glare of a condemned man.

"Come on, Monty!" Esmé shouted. "Get the key!"

"I'm looking, I'm looking!" said Monty, as he frantically searched all of his pockets, at last finding the key in his jacket. He handed

it to Keith, who slotted the key into the outside lock and opened the lid. Potty used all his force to mount the transparent step inside the tank. Finally, he raised his head above the water.

Potty gasped – loud and long.

"Thank goodness!" said Esmé.

"Sorry if I delayed things," said Monty. "I'm so glad you're OK, Potty."

Potty gasped again, water dripping off his nose, his face now returning to its usual colour.

"I'll get you a towel," said Esmé, running backstage.

"What… on… earth?" Keith was completely and absolutely bewildered by the failure of the inside lock. "I checked and double checked everything last night. The catch should have opened easily."

"Well, it didn't," said Esmé, handing a towel to Potty who had just hauled himself out of the tank.

"I just don't know what happened…" Keith found a chair and started inspecting the lid of the tank.

After a moment Keith spoke. "The catch has been removed," he said, still baffled.

"No!" exclaimed Potty, and shivered.

"Is it me, or is the tank leaking?" asked Monty, as he looked at the ever-increasing pool of water around the tank.

"Not *another* problem," sighed Keith, checking for holes in the tank. "This is not the best start to the rehearsals. Ah, I've got

it, *here*." He pointed to a small, perfectly round hole towards the bottom of the side panel. "Looks like it was made by a drill. Maybe I did it by mistake…"

But most likely not, thought Esmé, full of suspicion.

"This reminds me of my houseboat days…" Potty reminisced. "I discovered a leak and Shep the beetle had to learn the breaststroke in ten seconds. But it wasn't sabotage, it was just a very old boat."

"We'd better mop up the water right away," said Esmé. "It's going to damage the footlights – maybe more."

There was a noise of a door slamming.

"*What's* damaged?" asked Tabitha, walking purposefully into the auditorium with Twinkle.

The trouble with the Sea Spray was that all visitors could see and hear what was going before those on stage had noticed anyone arrive.

"Oh, my diddly dee!" cried Twinkle, rushing on to the stage, russet-coloured chiffon flowing behind her like a keen ghost. "What have you people done to our lovely theatre?"

"Not to worry," said Monty brightly, trying to placate the Table sisters. "We're used to Potty's mess – in fact we've cleaned up after him many times before."

"*Many times before?*" asked Tabitha, horrified. "You mean this happens constantly?"

"Oh, deary," said Twinkle. "Not *today*…"

Potty opened his dripping arms out wide.

"Rest assured, fine gentlewomen. I must concede, we have just had a technical hitch but I can promise that we will not let this small hiccup ruin your building, or the show."

Tabitha crossed her arms.

"Well, you'll have to be quick," she said, jaw clenched. "Mr Portobello has just phoned us – he's due here in ten minutes to inspect the theatre in order to build his bid. We simply must have this place spick and span by then."

An excerpt from

Dr Pompkins – Totality Magic

TRICK: Card Command

This is a short trick that will take minutes to learn, and never fails to impress the gentlefolk.

Take a pack of cards and find the Queen of Hearts. Place the card between thumb and index finger in your right hand, and raise that hand above your head.

Confidently inform your audience (of gentlefolk, that is) that the card is completely under your command, and will do anything you tell it to.

Now fling the card upwards, saying, "Card, I order you to come down!" or similar and, true to your will, it will do so every time. Hah hah!

———

Unless you have jam on your fingers, or glue.

Secrets

A magician is only as good as his or her secrets. If you *have* detailed your tricks in a notebook, keep it locked (as mentioned previously). Similarly, do not start revealing anything, even when you are talking to friends over coffee, not even fellow magicians. You have to be cunning, you have to be wily. Never disclose your tricks to a soul. A good friend of mine, Mr Pat Daniels, once thought it safe to tell a passing dog about a new card trick and in no time the pup – Mr Chihuahua – had become a worldwide success on the magic circuit.

In all totality,

Dr Pompkins

CHAPTER SEVEN

Luxury Yacht

It was not a particularly bright or fine morning, but as Mr Portobello made his way up the beach to the Sea Spray Theatre he had a spring in his step. His meeting with his accountant and friend, David Dinner, had gone well. Mr Portobello was now sure that the plan of action they had put in place would mean that the Sea Spray Theatre would soon be his, quickly and – most importantly – cheaply.

"I need the show to fail, David," Mr Portobello had explained, "or else people will flock to the Sea Spray and Potty will become a roaring success. Then the Table sisters will ask for a *proper* amount of money for the theatre, which I just don't want to pay."

Mr Portobello had paused, imagining a fat pile of money leaving his bank account.

"To make matters worse," the businessman had continued, "Keith Chalk is now helping Potty build the props for his act. The show is going from strength to strength. We need to work out how I can still buy the theatre for peanuts, in order to knock it down and build my amusement arcade."

"Hmm…" David Dinner had replied, picking

up a toothpick from his desk and starting to chew. "Let's go through the figures – what's the *lowest* offer we could make?"

"A pound?"

David had sighed and the toothpick fallen out of his mouth on to the carpeted floor. "Come on, Mr Portobello, be sensible."

In a surprising turn of events, David Dinner had picked the toothpick off the floor and put it back between his yellowing teeth.

"You must remember," said David, chewing slowly, "that this is exactly the same thing that happened with Gary Meringue. We thought that there was no way we could ruin that show, but we managed to… *deal* with him."

"I suppose we did…" said Mr Portobello.

"And even the police have stopped asking questions now," added David. "He's just another missing person. A misadventure at sea…"

"He's very well behaved," replied Mr Portobello. "I never hear a squeak out of him."

"That's good," replied David. "Have you thought of inviting Potty back to Crab Pie Island? If so, you could, um, *detain* him for a while…"

"Well, of course I will if I have to, but the difference with Gary Meringue was that he didn't have a niece and nephew with him," said Mr Portobello. "He worked alone… but I can see those pesky Pepper children will make a nuisance of themselves if anything happens to their precious uncle."

David had finally taken the pick out of his mouth and poured himself a cup of instant coffee from the pot on the side table. He had offered some to Mr Portobello, served in a chipped porcelain mug that had 'Disco Daze' printed on it.

"No, thanks," said Mr Portobello. "It will keep me awake all night."

"Suit yourself," replied David, who started sipping his hot drink rather loudly. "It seems to me that you need some simple sabotage in the meantime. Just to be getting along with. Then if that doesn't work, you know what to do."

At which point David had raised his right eyebrow, knowingly.

Mr Portobello smiled to himself as he remembered the conversation. Mounting the theatre steps, he felt smug in the knowledge that his new plan had already been put into action. This morning he would make a cursory inspection of the Sea Spray knowing full well the scene that would greet him.

Mr Portobello was pleased to be right. Absolutely chuffed to bits. Before him was a picture of devastation. The stage floor was covered in water, despite the best efforts of everyone to clean it up. There was a huge plastic tank on its side with pieces of metal strewn everywhere. The Potty Magician was sneezing in a corner, drinking from a mug of hot cocoa as his niece and nephew fussed around him.

"Oh, dear," said Mr Portobello, knowing this was the bedlam he had helped to create.

"It might look like a complete catastrophe, Mr Portobello," Twinkle rushed up greet the visitor, "but we'll have this cleaned up in an instant."

"As soon as you can say 'Abracadabra'," added Tabitha, ardently.

"You should have seen the place half an hour ago," said Keith. "We've made great inroads and we're all sure that if we pull together, we'll have the stage in a better state than it was in before."

Mr Portobello stopped and surveyed the devastation. Yes, it was bad, but something else started to niggle. Instead of wallowing in dejection, Potty's team seemed to be *rising to the challenge*.

"Have you got a dustpan, Tabitha?" Esmé asked as Tabitha mopped and Potty blow-dried the floorboards with a hairdryer. Keith was fiddling about with a screwdriver and the footlights while Twinkle and Monty together pushed the tank upright.

"I say only ten minutes until the next pot of tea!" laughed Potty, to which Twinkle made a joke about "Pott-tea" and everyone giggled.

Mr Portobello's smug satisfaction drained from him faster than the water from the fish tank. He thought back to his conversation with David Dinner. If Plan A wasn't working, he must resort to Plan B…

"Ahem," he cleared his throat. "Why don't you lot take a break and come over to Crab Pie Island for a bit? Forget about the mess – relax and recuperate," Mr Portobello purred, slicking back his oil-slick hair.

"But we need to finish cleaning up," said Esmé.

"The Table girls can do that," answered Mr Portobello. "Tabs – you will, won't you?"

Tabitha – on hearing that she was now being called 'Tabs' – winced. Twinkle looked over at her as if to say, '*Now you know how it feels.*'

"I'm certain that Keith has the resources to fix the tank back at his workshop at Crab Pie," continued Mr Portobello. "That way,

everyone's a winner," he laughed lightly, for effect, then wished he'd cleaned his teeth this morning.

Esmé looked at Mr Portobello suspiciously. *How does he know it was the tank that was the problem?* she wondered.

"I need to sit down, dear," Twinkle suddenly announced. "I'm having one of my turns."

Indeed, Twinkle Table's nose was twitching. Monty grabbed her a chair from the wings.

"Are you all right, Twinkle?" asked Keith. "Can I get you some water?"

"I can see another image… another vision…" said Twinkle in a low voice, eyes closed, chin on her chest.

Her head leant from side to side and her knees knocked together. Esmé was sure her ears started wiggling too.

"*Woooah!*" she murmured.

"Oh, dear," said Tabitha. "This is her fourth vision in as many days."

"*Murghhhh…*" Twinkle's head rolled around a little more.

"She's certainly having a bumper time of it."

"*Fluuuuurgh…* I'm seeing a well-stocked fridge… and a packet of cheddar cheese," mumbled Twinkle.

"Cheddar?" asked Tabitha. "Can you be so sure?"

"Oh, yes," said Twinkle, head rolling around some more. "Oh, *yeeeees.*"

Twinkle murmured again as Tabitha suddenly held her fingers over her temples.

"*Ooh!*" Tabitha quivered. "*Wooah!*"

She grabbed Twinkle's chair, as if she were about to faint.

"Someone, please, I also need a chair. I'm going under as well…"

"Are you having a vision too?" asked Monty. "How exciting. Two at once!"

"Golly, I mean… gosh… I think… *Drooooouuu hurgle…*" Tabitha's nose started twitching and her head moved slowly from one side to the other. Her feet shuffled and her mouth pursed.

"A picture is forming in my mind…" whispered Tabitha, deeply. "It's the face of… David Beckham… Ooh, no, it's not. It's the

117

magician Gary Meringue! He's hovering above us. He's talking... But these are words I cannot quite make out."

"Cheddar!" murmured Twinkle, happily.

"Meringue," muttered Tabitha.

"Cheddar," slurred Twinkle.

"It's definitely Meringue," croaked Tabitha and at once both ladies raised their hands straight ahead of them – and suddenly dropped them again.

There was silence.

Esmé had never seen anything like it. Monty had *almost* seen something like it on a TV programme but Mr and Mrs Pepper had told him it was too late and sent him off to bed. Potty had definitely seen something like it in 1972 when a well-known illusionist had skilfully hypnotised two Collie dogs and made them both speak Japanese.

The businessman, however, was not impressed. "Come on, you old dears." He walked up the Tables and tapped both of them gently on the shoulder. "Wakey, wakey, rise and shine…"

Esmé did not like the way Mr Portobello spoke to them; it did not seem… respectful.

"Mr Portobello, they may have genuinely experienced some sort of spiritual phenomenon," she said.

In reply, Mr Portobello peered at Esmé, aghast that a *child* was talking back to an *adult*. However, he tried to conceal his astonishment.

"Charming girl," he said instead, pinching

Esmé's cheeks. "You are probably, er, right."

"CHEDDAR!" shouted Twinkle once last time. Esmé jumped in surprise – and both sisters came to with a jolt.

Tabitha checked herself, looking down at her feet and feeling for her arms. "I cannot believe it," she said. "I saw a vision too."

"Yes, I know," replied Twinkle. "Maybe it's the stress."

"I think *everyone* here is under a lot of stress." Mr Portobello turned to Potty. "Let's not waste any more time. The boat is waiting – let's go to Crab Pie Island right away."

"The boat I arrived in this morning?" asked Keith. "There's no mooring rope."

"Oh, really? I wonder how that happened?" said Mr Portobello innocently. "Don't worry, we'll take my yacht. Plenty of room for everyone."

"Splendid," said Potty, who was in excellent spirits. "It would be great to see your workshop, Keith."

"And we do need to get the fishbowl fixed, I suppose," said Esmé cautiously, though deep down she had a bad feeling about the trip.

Mr Portobello led the way out of the theatre, down the steps and on to the boat. Keith, Potty and Monty followed behind him, carrying the broken tank. The sky was brooding – even the seagulls were starting to take cover.

"An *interesting* weather front," remarked Potty as they boarded the boat. "There may

be no time for sunbathing."

"Mr Portobello, what's the difference between a boat and a yacht?" asked Monty as they prepared to leave for Crab Pie Island.

"Um… something to do with the… er, front bit," replied Mr Portobello. "And the rate of c-force to dyno-knots."

"Marvellous," said Potty. "Let's go."

As the boat moved away, the skies darkened further and the sea became a little moody. Although Crab Pie Island was only a mile or so from the shore, they were sailing against the wind, which was certainly not going to help the journey.

"Will we be all right in this weather?" Esmé asked Mr Portobello. "It is rather windy."

"No *problemo*," answered Mr Portobello.

"This boat is sturdy and strong. It can handle anything."

"Maybe we'll be stranded on the island!" laughed Monty.

Esmé glared at her brother. She didn't want to be stranded anywhere. They had a show to do.

"What is this yacht called, Mr Portobello?" asked Monty. "They all have names, don't they? Like the *Sultan of Speed* or *The Oceanic Administrator.*"

"It's called *The Titanic*, actually. Ha ha hah!" answered Mr Portobello, taking the helm.

As the boat moved slowly forwards the waves got larger and the yacht began to yaw from side to side. Monty and Esmé held on

tightly to the sides – and Keith gripped on to the tank. Sheets of icy rain began to fall from the dark skies. Thunder clapped. Esmé shivered next to Monty.

Despite what was going on around him, Mr Portobello appeared not to notice the storm and started to whistle as he steered the yacht through the hellish seas.

Esmé found this mostly peculiar. And slightly annoying.

Mr Portobello whistled a little more then shouted across to a wind-whipped Potty, "Do you ever worry about accidents at sea, Potts?"

Potty was matter-of-fact.

"No, I lived on a houseboat for many years. I never worry about the water."

"Oh, well, that's… good," replied Mr Portobello, his nasal hair swirling in the harsh sea air.

A wave approached. A large wave. An enormous wave. It hurtled towards the boat, a huge sodden blanket of disaster.

"*Wooargh!*" said Mr Portobello.

The boat rolled to one side. Keith held on to the tank as hard as he could as everyone else gripped on to their seats. The boat almost flipped over but at the last moment it quickly reverted back to the horizontal with a watery thud.

The wave hurtled past, looking for new disasters. Esmé, Monty, Potty and Keith breathed very real sighs of relief.

"That was a close one," said Mr Portobello,

125

although he laughed as he spoke. "Still here, Potty?"

A few minutes later, the yacht was safely docked at the island. But Esmé had an uneasy feeling. *Why was Mr Portobello laughing like that?* Esmé knew something was wrong but she just wasn't sure what. She knew one thing though – she did not trust Mr Portobello one bit.

An excerpt from

Dr Pompkins – Totality Magic

TRICK: The Unpoppable Balloon

Show your friends a fully blown-up balloon, then remark how you will be able to stick a pin into it without it deflating!

The secret is to prepare your balloon first with sticky tape – take a few small pieces and stick them on, making sure each does not wrinkle.

If you stick a pin through the centre of the tape, the balloon will not pop.

A balloon with a patterned surface will keep the sticky tape at its most invisible.

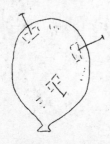

Party Magic

If your friends have enjoyed your table-top magic, they may ask you to put on a show at a party. At small parties you can perform close-up magic, but if there are lots of people you should put on a proper stage act.

Tips to remember:

There will always be people who will ask you to keep on doing more and more tricks, but it is better to do a short routine, finishing with a really strong effect – then you can save some of your surprises for the next party.

Remember that the most popular tricks are those in which the spectators take part. Welcome their input. Savour the joy. Maybe they will give you an extra cream bun and a glass of cherry pop for all your effort.

In all totality,

Dr Pompkins

CHAPTER EIGHT

Crab Pie Island

The storm had reduced visibility so greatly that it was only when the visitors moored by the beach that they saw what a strange house Mr Portobello lived in. As Mr Portobello ushered them through a door in an imposing metal fence, a peculiar, towering building emerged out of the sand. The house was puzzling – the ground floor was a modest size and was connected to Keith's workshop – but as the building continued upwards to the fourth floor it became wider. It was like an upside-down wedding cake.

At the very top of the building the windows were tiny and protected each by a metal grille. Esmé frowned at the strange house. *Wouldn't you want* big *windows on the top floor?* she thought to herself. The view must be amazing from up there…

"Whaddya think?" asked Mr Portobello as he led the visitors in.

"Fit for a king," said Potty, impressed. "*Topsy turvy.*"

"I'm delighted to have you here," said Mr Portobello, grinning at Potty in particular.

"I'll give you all a swift tour of the house," he continued, "which will give Keith time to rebuild the goldfish bowl in the workshop…"

The first floor living room housed a big TV screen, a big sofa and a big fluffy rug. "There's also a central remote control," explained Mr Portobello, "which controls the lighting, the heating, the telly, the stereo and the sea."

"The sea?" asked Uncle Potty.

"Just another joke," answered Mr Portobello, with a viscous glug of laughter in his voice.

Esmé wasn't impressed. She thought it was silly how Mr Portobello was so proud of his furniture and his gadgets. *Some grown-ups pay too much attention to things and what they are worth.*

On the second floor was Mr Portobello's bedroom, inside it a big wardrobe. Mr Portobello started droning on and on about 'fixtures', as if anyone was interested. "This shower unit," he said as they were shown the bathroom, "has a strong, steady 2.3ml flow and the thermostat was made in Germany to exacting standards. The faucets are made in Sweden by a former gymnast, which is why they're so bendy."

Potty raised an eyebrow to show interest, although even his attention was starting to wane by this point.

The third floor was empty but for a gleaming exercise bike. It had a breathtaking view of the sea and Crab Pie shore.

Esmé and Monty were entranced by the ocean, watching as the waves leapt and licked at the shore. The sky was a dark purple now, with small shards of daylight

breaking through the clouds. The pier was illuminated by beads of white light and a large glowing "Crab Pie" sign. In the town, the lumionous rectangles of shopfronts and sitting rooms shone back at them. Esmé wondered about all the creatures in the sea: the whales that understood certain words and all the different types of fish that didn't care about Mr Portobello's money. There were important seaweeds and corals that helped sustain the planet that would never notice if he bought another expensive sofa or not.

There was a shuffling sound.

"What's that funny noise?" asked Monty.

"Let's go downstairs," said Mr Portobello abruptly.

The shuffling started again.

"Is it coming from upstairs?" asked Esmé, straining to hear.

"Oh, no, it's the wind," replied Mr Portobello hastily, guiding his visitors back down the stairs. "Let's have a look at Keith's workshop and see how he's getting on."

Keith swept his hair back from his face as he finished fixing the hole in the tank. "Almost there," he said, pleased to see them. "Come in."

Esmé, Monty and Potty stepped into the workshop from the corridor that led to Mr Portobello's kitchen. In it were housed all sorts of machines. Some were lit with small flashing bulbs, others made faint bleeping

noises. Potty went up to a tall gadget that looked like an old-fashioned set of weighing scales.

"What's this?" he asked, tapping the machine.

"It's the banana-powered Test Your Strength Machine," said Keith.

"Go on, Potts, try your strength," interjected Mr Portobello. "Put a 'nana in the funnel and then punch the red disc as hard as you can."

Potty did as instructed. There was a whirring sound and the banana travelled down the small funnel and disappeared into the heart of the machine. Potty raised his right fist and then landed a punch on the red disc – *booph!* The machine whirred once more.

There was one long beep and then a small card popped out.

"Weakling," read Potty as he took the card, dismayed.

Monty giggled.

"You can't argue with that, Pottsville," replied Mr Portobello.

"Is this a fruit machine?" asked Monty, who walked up to another bulky object. The front panel was lit in a studied assortment of bright, citrus colours and there were pictures of fruit doing some sort of a dance along the top of the display.

"It's the One-Armed-Bandit Smoothie Machine," said Keith.

"Try your luck," Mr Portobello said loudly,

fishing in his jacket pocket to produce a metal token. Monty took the coin and put it in the slot.

"Now pull the lever," said Mr Portobello.

The machine was very old and, although it had been modernised, its mechanisms were stiff. Monty tried hard but it took four attempts before the lever creaked downwards.

Drrriiiing! came a bell and three fruity discs spun in the centre of the machine.

Dring! The image of a smiling apple appeared. *Dring!* A pear. Next, a lemon.

There was a gurgling behind the machine and in twenty-two seconds (Esmé counted) a dark brown drink appeared in a window, just like a vending machine.

"A fruit smoothie," said Mr Portobello.

"Fantastic. Get your five a day the easy way – you need your vitamins, Monty."

"But it looks like cola," said Monty, taking the glass.

"It smells like cola," said Esmé, sniffing.

"Well," Keith started to explain. "You're right in a wa—"

Mr Portobello was quick to interrupt. "No, no, it's all fruity," he explained. "Nothing artificial."

Keith said nothing, but plucked two straws from behind the machine and the Pepper twins shared the drink. It was definitely cola.

The longer she stayed in the room, the more Esmé wondered about the machines. All the inventions seemed to be based on arcade games. *Why is Mr Portobello so interested in slot machines?* she wondered. Esmé had that uneasy feeling again. She looked at her watch, a new Timex to replace her old one that had been stuffed inside a tangerine and ruined during one of Potty's more experimental tricks.

"It's getting late," she said. "We need to get back to the Sea Spray and continue rehearsals."

"Come into the kitchen and have a quick cup of tea before you go," suggested Mr Portobello.

"Splendid idea!" said Potty, before Esmé could stop him.

Bleep! Dee-blee-gleep!

As they walked along the corridor towards

141

the kitchen another impressive machine blocked their way. It was bigger than any of the others they had seen.

"What's that?" asked Monty.

"Oh, that's a Giant Penny Fall – nothing, really. Come and have a cup of tea," said Mr Portobello nervously.

"It's got so big I can't squeeze it back through the workshop door," explained Keith. "I added the giant pincer you asked for, Mr Portobello, but now it's stuck out here in the hallway."

The Giant Penny Fall was an extra-large version of those machines in amusement arcades that you put coins into to try and push other coins off the ledge. Esmé remembered spending an hour on such a device, convinced that with the next 'push' she was going to get a hundred pounds' worth of loose change – either that or a bright green teddy bear. But nothing happened at all that day – the pushing mechanism continued to push, the coins hardly moved, and the pincer never grabbed the bear. Esmé had disliked arcade games from that moment onward.

"It's an impressive machine," said Potty, full of admiration. "What's it for?"

"Er, um… it's just for decoration," answered Mr Portobello, awkwardly. "Nothing a talented magician like you would be interested in."

Esmé didn't like the machine and its giant pincer one bit. "Look, we've had a great afternoon," she said, walking towards the

front door, "but *surely* it's time to go. Now the tank's been mended we've got to take it back and rehearse for the show."

"I'm ever so hungry," announced Mr Portobello, strolling into the kitchen and opening the fridge door. "How about sandwiches?"

"Well, I must say that sounds like a superb idea," said Potty, following him. "I'm famished." Esmé cringed – Mr Portobello was stalling for time. Monty and Keith also walked into the kitchen, forcing Esmé to join them – she couldn't keep standing in the hall on her own.

"You're very kind," Esmé told Mr Portobello. "But it's too much effort for you."

"I was going to get Keith to do it," he

replied. "Hah, hah, just joking, Keith."

"I'm hungry too," Monty piped up.

"Well, let's all eat!" said Mr Portobello.

Esmé wished that Monty and Potty would realise that they needed to get back to the theatre straight away.

"Could we take the sandwiches to eat in the boat on the way back instead?" she asked.

"In this weather?" remarked Mr Portobello, pointing out of the kitchen window at the still-stormy seas. "They would get soggy."

"You said that you have plenty of boats," said Monty, who had noticed the expression on Esmé's face and remembered that they still had more rehearsals before the show opened. "My sister's right, we still have a lot

145

to do at the theatre. Have you something with a roof on it?"

"A roof..." mused Mr Portobello. "Hmm, yes, good idea. You and Esmé can go on the smaller boat, it's completely covered. Keith can take you back."

"Is it safe?" asked Esmé, remembering their traumatic journey to the island.

"Oh, yes, it's a much better boat than the yacht," replied Keith.

"However," said Mr Portobello, sucking his teeth and remembering his Plan B, "it means there won't be room for all of us... So I suggest that the Potty Magician and I go back on my super-quick speedboat."

"Ooh," said Potty, rather excited by the idea of a faster journey.

"And the sandwiches?" asked Monty.

"Yes, we can enjoy them on the way, in our own *separate* sea vehicles…" Mr Portobello grinned and seemed extra-specially pleased. "I've got some crisps too… Cheddar cheese?" said Mr Portobello as he handed the sandwiches out.

Esmé's ears pricked up. *Cheddar cheese! Wasn't this the phrase that Twinkle Table had shouted out in her trance? And if so, what significance did it have?*

"Come on, let's go," Esmé said, determined now to get them out of there. Keith led the way to the boatyard.

Before them were three boats – the 'Titanic' yacht, the speedboat and a normal covered boat. Esmé and Monty followed

closely behind Keith and boarded the covered boat.

"You will come straight after us, won't you?" asked Esmé.

"Of course! We'll be right behind you," said Mr Portobello.

In a few moments the Pepper twins were roaring off to the pier. "This boat is easier to handle than the last one," Keith called back from the helm. "I think this journey will be less eventful."

Esmé looked back and waved goodbye to Potty, but he and Mr Portobello were deep in conversation and not yet on the speedboat. Mr Portobello seemed to be trying to get Potty back into the house. *What was happening?*

"Look at the island," Esmé said to Monty. "Something isn't right. They're not getting on the other boat. Keith, we have to turn the boat around right now."

"I'm afraid that's impossible – the wind is too strong in the northerly direction," replied Keith. "It's fine going this way because the wind is pushing us along but we won't be able to go back until it dies down… which won't be for hours."

"Maybe they are just getting some more cheese sandwiches?" reasoned Monty.

"Maybe," said Esmé, but in her heart she didn't believe it.

An excerpt from

Dr Pompkins – Totality Magic

TRICK: Break the Matchstick

Ask a friend to hold an ordinary matchstick between the fingers of one hand, so it rests over the middle finger {see fig. 1}.

The challenge is to keep the fingers of the hand straight, and break the match. Impossible, gadzooks!

The match will not break if placed the way shown.

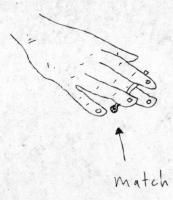

match

Of Magic Words and Actions

We have listed before the fact that you can use a catchphrase, if you like that sort of thing. Magic words, such as the famed 'abracadabra' are also part of this. But recently people have foregone this idea and think modernity means brooding, sulky silence. Nonsense! If you want a word to say when you perform your little miracles, Pompkins says, *go ahead*! Why not say, 'Havanabanana!', for instance, when clear water turns yellow in a glass tumbler? Why not shout, 'I-Am-Personally-Confused-By-Pencils!' when, during your trick, you change a rabbit into a pencil? Just a thought.

In all totality,

Dr Pompkins

CHAPTER NINE

Pier Again

As Keith moored the boat by Crab Pie Pier – a little more successfully this time – Esmé and Monty looked up to see the Table sisters running down to meet them.

"You're back!" shouted Twinkle, chiffon waving wildly around the top of her head.

"We found these," said a breathless Tabitha, running up after her sister with one of Potty's posters in hand. "Look."

Esmé took the poster and saw, scrawled

across it in red marker pen, the word 'cancelled'.

"What does this mean?" asked Esmé, bewildered. "Who wrote this?"

"I was going to ask you the same thing," said Tabitha. "All the posters along the pier have been scribbled on like this."

"*Is* the show cancelled?" asked Twinkle.

"Where's Potty?" asked Tabitha.

"He's still on the island," answered Esmé. "He was just about to board Mr Portobello's speedboat when we left, but then I saw him go back inside the house."

"Oh," said Tabitha, confused. "But Potty *is* coming, isn't he? Are you sure he doesn't want to cancel the show?"

"Absolutely certain," said Keith. "We've

talked about nothing else."

"Why don't we give Mr Portobello a call," suggested Tabitha, motioning towards the gypsy caravan. "Find out where Potty is."

So Keith, the Pepper twins and the Table sisters hurried down the pier to use the phone in the caravan. They managed to squeeze themselves in, then waited in tense silence as Twinkle went into the back to make the call.

"Mr Portobello, yes, hello, yes, Twinkle Table... Yes, *Twinks*... Just wondering where Potty had got to... Right, oh. *Oh*... Yes, goodbye."

"According to Mr Portobello," Twinkle said as she came out to join them, "Potty made his own way here by speedboat, following straight after you. Mr Portobello was surprised that Potty hadn't yet arrived."

"But I saw them go into the house…" replied Esmé. "Potty *didn't* make his own way here."

"Then it can only mean one thing," said Tabitha. "Mr Portobello is lying."

There was silence in the caravan for a moment as everyone absorbed the news. Monty was first to speak.

"What are we going to do?" He looked across at his sister.

Twinkle started to reply: "Well, I could look at the tea—"

But Esmé interrupted.

"If we were in this situation back at home I would go straight to the CostSnippas

155

Convenience Store and ask Jimi Sinha for advice," she said. "He'd know what to do."

Monty immediately felt a sharp pang for home. "I wish Jimi was here. He helped us save the International Magic Guys – I'm sure he could help save Potty too."

"I know – let's phone him," said Esmé. "Explain the situation, maybe he'll be able to help."

"It's worth a try…" said Monty, perking up a bit.

The Table Sisters nodded. "Please, use our phone. We'll wait outside while you make the call."

A few minutes later Esmé came running out of the caravan, wearing a huge smile.

"They're coming," she yelled, jumping up and down. "Jimi and the International Magic Guys are coming to save Potty!"

Dr Pompkins – Totality Magic

TRICK: Vanishing Sugar Lumps

You will need two sugar lumps for this trick. Firstly, drape a paper napkin over your half-closed fist. Then, with the fingers of your other hand, push down the centre of the napkin to make a 'well'.

Drop the sugar lumps into the well and sprinkle some salt over the napkin. Quickly tear up the napkin into small pieces, showing the sugar lumps have disappeared.

The secret is to push a hole right through the paper and then let the sugar lumps fall through it on to your lap as you reach for the salt cellar {see fig. 1}.

Ingeniosity!

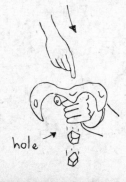

hole

Television

Much has been made of television magic and its ability to impress the audience with what is not only the magician's skill but what can also be editing techniques and camera angles etc. I, myself, do not stand for such modern ideas and prefer to perform my shows to real live people who sit in drawing rooms and look smart. When offered a high-profile show on TV (as it is called), I always say no. Keep magic live! Keep it real. Unless you are offered more than £5, I would say to your TV person, 'No, thanks,' and I would say it in a French accent – just to show you mean business.

In some confusion over accents,

Dr Pompkins

CHAPTER TEN

Potty and the
Failed Distraction

"Can I just ask why I'm here?" Potty asked Mr Portobello, quite politely, wishing that he'd trained as an escapologist rather than a stage magician. "I need to go back to the Sea Spray immediately."

"This is what I need to talk to you about," came the reply. "Excuse me."

Mr Portobello moved Potty out of the way of the fridge that he was chained to, opened

the door and took out a packet of Chantenay carrots (the small ones with lots of flavour). He tore open the packet and proceeded to start snacking.

"Now, I hope you won't think me impolite, but I don't wish for you to perform this week. Or next. Maybe never. When is the show?"

"Day after tomorrow," said Potty.

Mr Portobello took a huge bite out of the small carrot and threw the uneaten stub out of the open kitchen window.

"Shame, really. That's the day I have to submit my *generous* offer to Tabitha and Twinkle. Dear ladies…" Mr Portobello trailed off. "But of course they are not dear ladies, are they? They are silly old women who have ludicrous fainting fits and expect a hideous price for their horrible old theatre."

"My show is not going to stop you making an offer," said Potty, trying to be calm. He did not like being chained to a fridge. It was cold and, besides, he was hungry.

"Your show is going to stop me making a *low* offer," replied Mr Portobello, throwing another carrot stub out of the window. "If you perform, you'll be a roaring success – and that can't happen. So, if I kidnap you, you *can't* perform – and the Tables will have no audience, no profit, no future. That's exactly what I want."

"You can't just keep me here!" said Potty, starting to become uncharacteristically irritable.

"Can't I?" smirked Mr Portobello. "The

163

Sea Spray Theatre is soon to become the Sea Spray Amusement Arcade," he continued, ignoring Potty. "Who wants to see your rotten performance when there are all sorts of exciting machines to lose money on? Who needs entertainment when people can give their hard-earned cash to me via my machines?"

Potty was starting to lose his cool.

"Look here, Mr Portobello," he said. "Your machines will wipe the soul out of Crab Pie Pier. The Sea Spray Theatre brings joy to everyone – young and old, tall and small… and anything in between. Now, I would like to go back to the theatre immediately. I'm done with this chat."

"Not possible, I'm afraid. I've told you,

you are being detained."

Mr Portobello had one last crunch of an especially small carrot and chucked the rest out of the window.

"But, Mr Portobello, I implore you. It's not only the show – young Esmé and Monty need me. I am looking after them while their parents are away."

The businessman rolled his eyes.

"You are becoming a little bit tiresome," he said, fishing in his trouser pocket for a key. "I think we'd better put you out of the way, rather than leave you chained to a fridge, yelling near some carrots."

Unlocking his shackles, Mr Portobello grasped Potty by the wrist and pulled him upstairs.

"*Ooof!*"

Potty tried to waggle his arms in order to pull off a masterful distraction technique but Mr Portobello's grip was too tight.

"Where are you taking me?" yelled Potty.

"Just follow me," said Mr Portobello, dragging Potty up four flights of stairs until they reached the top floor. Potty wiggled and tried to break free but he was having no luck.

"Gosh, you really are a weakling aren't you?" laughed Mr Portobello, ridiculing Potty's pathetic attempts at escape.

Potty was annoyed with himself. How had he got to the point where he was about to be incarcerated for ever in an island prison? He should have struggled more, put up a

greater fight, but it was too late. Or was it? *It's now or never*, thought Potty. *I must distract my captor in order to give me some time to escape.*

Potty managed to loosen an arm and place a hand in his waistcoat pocket to bring out the long length of tied silk scarves folded inside.

"Let the distraction commence!" he announced as the silk danced majestically in colourful arcs and... ended up tangled around Mr Portobello's legs.

"Get off!" cried Mr Portobello, stamping on the scarves and setting himself free.

There's only one thing for it, thought Potty. Potty wasn't a violent man – he hardly ever raised his voice – but he had to do something right away.

As the door before him opened, Potty raised his long, long right arm, moved his elbow back to carry the blow and put all his weight into it.

"*Kerrpow!*" said Potty as he triumphantly... cuffed the top of Mr Portobello's left ear, barely touching him.

"What are you doing, Potty?" gruffled Mr Portobello. He bundled Potty into the room and quickly locked the door behind him.

"I'll bring you some baked beans at about half past eight," Mr Portobello called through the keyhole. "There's a toilet to your right and I've made up the spare bed. Anything else, don't hesitate to shout. Well, *do* hesitate – I've got some important telly to watch."

In the dark room, Potty panicked and started knocking on the door.

"Let me out! Let me out, I tell you," he yelled, but Mr Portobello was already padding downstairs and had resolved to ignore any sound from the top floor.

Potty repeatedly pummelled the door but to no avail. He searched his waistcoat pockets for a torch, but instead he brought out a small plastic frog and two foam tadpoles.

"That's not what I need," said Potty, throwing them on the floor. "The foaming frogspawn trick is useless under these circumstances!"

Potty thought harder. "Maybe there's something to open the door with..." He fumbled about in his pockets some more but could only come up with a plastic spoon and a seven-sided die.

"Bother!" Potty exclaimed, falling to his knees.

"Bother indeed," said a voice in the darkness. "I've been trying to come up with a plan all year."

Potty turned, startled, and looked right into the blackness. "Who's there?"

"Gary Meringue," said the voice. "Pleased to meet you."

An excerpt from

Dr Pompkins – Totality Magic

TRICK: The Indestructible Banknote

To prepare, take a long brown envelope and cut a slit across the back.

Then hold the envelope with the slit towards you and slide a banknote into it, making sure that the bottom end comes through the slit at the back. Fold the note upwards {see figs. 1 and 2}.

Grab a pencil and swiftly push it through the slit – so that it looks as if you are going right through the note.

All you have to do now is pull the note out of the envelope – it is, of course, completely untouched.

Et merci.

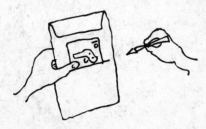

Magic Shops

Some of the finest tricks and apparatus you will find in the magic shop are those which are the most traditional, through and through. Examples are the ball vase, which makes a red ball vanish and reappear. You may recognise the magic paddles, which flip to reveal and thence to hide those cheeky black spots. The imp bottle is famous – it will only 'lie down' at the magician's command – but it is a quick and simple trick for a train journey or the top of a mountain. All these (tricks, not mountains) are sold in their thousands every year, delighting generation upon generation. Never feel the classics are outmoded; their charm will last and last.

In all totality,

Dr Pompkins

CHAPTER ELEVEN

The International Magic Guys

"You haven't actually told us who these International Magic Guys are," said Twinkle, as she put on the kettle in the caravan. Team Potty – the Pepper twins, the Table sisters and Keith – was having a cup of tea after a long day of tearing down posters.

Esmé and Monty both began to explain at once about the IMG and last year's summer show that had saved the club from ruin.

Monty and Esmé both spoke over each other in their eagerness to explain.

"Deidre Lemons used to have a white tiger called Dennis but now she has a rabbit called Bernard which she carries with her wherever she goes…"

"The Great Stupeedo is the best human cannonball that has ever lived…"

"Clive Pastel can levitate *and* juggle at the same time…"

"And once, Maureen Houdini got herself locked in a trunk and couldn't get out…"

Just then, they heard an enormous clattering noise. Looking out of the caravan window they saw a huge silver helicopter in the sky above Crab Pie Pier. It hovered over the

theatre and then landed on the steel roof of the *Roses and Noses* tattoo parlour.

The twins, the Table sisters and Keith Chalk ran excitedly out of the caravan and down the beach to meet them. "You're here!" exclaimed Esmé as Clive Pastel, Deidre Lemons, Bernard the rabbit, the Great Stupeedo, Maureen Houdini and catering ace Jimi Sinha emerged one by one from the helicopter and wobbled down the parlour's wonky fire escape.

"Where did you find the helicopter?" Monty asked Maureen Houdini.

"It belongs to Clive," Maureen replied. "He's made it big in Las Vegas."

"Esmé and Monty Pepper!" cried Deidre running – with Bernard in her arms – to hug

the twins. "How are you? In a spot of bother over Potty?"

The Great Stupeedo came over and shook hands with the Table sisters and Keith Chalk. "Pleased to meet you. If you ever need someone shot out of a cannon, I'm your man."

"I told everyone what had happened," explained Jimi.

"Great – now we can act fast," said Esmé. "I think Potty could be in real danger."

"It sounds like we need to act right away," said the Great Stupeedo, taking his helmet hanging from his waistband and putting it on his head. "I, for one, am ready."

Esmé looked out to sea – it was now almost calm. The night was dark and Mr Portobello, she hoped, would not be expecting them…

Within minutes they had formulated a plan. Esmé read the notes to everyone:

"One: we fly over in Clive's helicopter.

Two: we break into Mr Portobello's house.

Three: we find Potty and rescue him!

Any questions?"

"How will we break into the house without getting noticed?" asked Monty.

"We can all use our skills to help," said Deidre. "Myself and Bernard can squeeze through small spaces – although I must say Bernard has been getting a little tubby of late so he might need more of a shove."

"I can use my escapology skills to open any locked doors," said Maureen.

"I can be launched from anywhere, into

179

anything," said Stupeedo. "It's very handy."

"And I'll fly the helicopter," added Clive.

"Monty and I already know the layout of the house," said Esmé. "We'll search for Potty once we're all in."

All eyes turned to Keith. He was silent at first, then asked, "Would any of you mind if I stayed behind? I'd like to set up the goldfish bowl and fix the pyrotechnics. I can do it all if given a few hours. We've all got to remember there's a show to be performed the day after tomorrow."

They all nodded in agreement.

"I'd like to source some local ingredients for the best Global Snack Trolley ever," said Jimi Sinha. "A good magic show needs good snacks."

"And myself and Twinkle will stick up some new posters," said Tabitha. "The show must go on!"

"Hurray!" they all shouted in unison.

"Right then, there's not a moment to lose – let's go!" said Esmé, and without further delay they piled into Clive's helicopter.

Dr Pompkins – Totality Magic

TRICK: The Floating Sausage

Hold your forefingers together in front of your face, about ten centimetres away from your eyes.

Don't stare too hard and you will see what looks like a 'sausage' shape in between your fingertips.

Separate your fingers slightly and the 'sausage' will seem to float in the air.

***

Now, remember – you cannot eat it with beans and chips, hah hah. Which reminds me, I am due a Danish pastry about this time.

Design a Magic Poster

Historically, all the greats of magic promoted their work through posters, which advertised the times and details of each show. Original posters are now worth thousands of pounds and are beautiful in design and print. Now, you must design your own! Refine the layout carefully in pencil first, decide what name you will go by, fill in the image with poster paints, and use a felt tip for smaller lettering. The word "MAGIC" should always be in capital letters so that everyone notices it. Use a simple image like cards, hands or a rabbit, and don't use too many colours. A combination of red, yellow and black is one of the most effective. Even if this is just for your bedroom wall, to remind yourself to practise your craft, I urge you to do yours today.

Pens aloft in all totality,

Dr Pompkins

CHAPTER TWELVE

Operation Potty

As Esmé and Monty climbed inside the helicopter and strapped themselves into their seats behind Clive and the empty co-pilot's space, they felt a rush of exhilaration.

Deidre was sat just behind them, cooing over Bernard who had a seat of his own next to hers. "He's still not right," she said. "I can tell something's up. He's so sleepy and he hasn't eaten for a whole day now."

Maureen and the Great Stupeedo took

their places in the back and mentally prepared themselves for the rescue by humming.

With a turbulous rumble and a droning grumble the helicopter shuddered into action. A moment later – albeit a rather jolting, jarring moment – the machine was up in the air.

As the helicopter gained height, it began to sway roughly from side to side. "It's quite wobbly, isn't it?" said Monty, holding tight.

"Yes, it's not as smooth as I imagined..." said Esmé.

"Oh, my goodness me!" shrieked Deidre.

"Try to calm down," said Stupeedo, who had stopped humming, sharpish. "It's only a bit of wind."

"No, it's not that!" yelled Deidre. "It's Bernard, I think he's just given birth."

All eyes turned to see Bernard with a small baby rabbit sitting next to him.

"Oh, my word," continued Deidre. "Another one! I need hot towels and brandy." Deidre instinctively unclipped herself from the seat and walked up to Clive at the front of the helicopter. "You do keep brandy in the glove compartment, don't you?"

"Please, Deidre, I'm trying to fly the helicopter," said Clive, whose hands were starting to tremble over the levers. "It requires a lot of concentration."

"Do sit down, Deidre," said Maureen. "Wait till we land."

"So is it a him, or is it a her?" asked Stupeedo.

"Ooh, there's another one," said Deidre, pacing about in the small space. "That's *three* babies. Now where *are* the towels?"

"I'm confused," said Stupeedo, leaning over to inspect Bernard and her babies. "Ooooo, aren't they cute?"

Clive looked back over his shoulder and caught a glimpse of Bernard giving birth. "*Eurgh!*" he wailed.

"Are you all right, Clive?" Maureen unclipped herself – if everyone else was up and about it she didn't see why she had to stay in her seat.

"Ooh, it's just... *pheurghle* – wind... rabbits... turbulence... *argh*... babies... clouds..." burbled Clive, looking distinctly unwell.

187

"You've gone green," Maureen told Clive.

"I *feel* green," replied Clive.

Esmé watched in horror as Clive started to hyperventilate.

"Has anyone got a paper bag?" asked Maureen. "Oh – what are we going to do? Clive's shivering all over!"

Esmé climbed over into the front to take a look at Clive. As she watched him, his eyes suddenly shut tight, his body juddered and then he flopped in his seat.

"He's fainted!" said Esmé, turning back to everyone.

Maureen prodded Clive's shoulder but he was out cold. The helicopter made a sudden swoop and a violent *whhoooorghhle*.

"We're all going to die!" yelled Monty as

the helicopter began to lose height rapidly and rush towards the water below.

Esmé grabbed the lever from Clive's limp hands and tried to hold the machine steady.

"What are we going to do now?" asked Stupeedo. "Who's gonna fly this thing?"

"Auto-pilot?" asked Deidre.

"Helicopters do not have autopilots," announced Maureen.

"Monty's right – we're doomed!" yelled Stupeedo. "Bagsy the ejector seat."

"Sit down, Stupeedo," ordered Maureen. "Where's the manual? Esmé, just hold it steady. That's it. You're doing a great job."

Deidre looked at Stupeedo, who threw a glance at Maureen, who shrugged her shoulders at Monty. Should they let this girl,

this small girl, fly the helicopter?

"Just keep doing what you're doing, Esmé," said Maureen. "Do you think you can fly this thing if we read to you from the manual?"

"I'm sure I can," said Esmé, who was shaking slightly as she settled herself in the empty co-pilot's seat. *How hard can it be?* she thought to herself. *Do it for Potty.*

"Here's the manual, Maureen," said Deidre, handing the *EeezyHover HC2100* guide over.

"OK," said Maureen. "You've got the collective control lever, now find the cyclic control with your right hand."

Esmé carefully grabbed the central lever with her other hand. The helicopter's frantic circular motion started to lose pace.

"Now, put your feet on the pedals – they control the tail rotor," said Monty, reading the manual over Maureen's shoulder. Esmé breathed in slowly and then out again and tried to feel for the right stability in the levers, which would maintain forward motion, height and level. Under Esmé's guidance, the helicopter finally stopped spinning and began to simply hover in the sky.

Maureen continued to read from the manual: "*Push the left pedal to increase the pitch of the tail rotor and turn to the left. Pushing the right pedal decreases the pitch and turns the helicopter to the right.*"

"Thanks, Maureen." Esmé gritted her teeth and pulled the collective control lever inward.

At last, as they made it across the water, Esmé gradually directed the helicopter downward (although it went upward at first) towards Crab Pie Island, without dipping the nose of the vehicle too much.

"You're doing well, Esmé," said Maureen. "Now, pull the collective control back – *ease gently to descend…*"

Carefully, Esmé did so and a moment later the helicopter thumped awkwardly on the ground, skidded forward a few metres, then came to rest.

"I don't quite believe it," said Maureen, loosening her collar. "Esmé, you've just successfully flown a helicopter!"

"Well done," said Monty, patting his sister enthusiastically on the back.

"Is Clive OK?" asked Deidre, looking at the slumped pilot.

Clive murmured and blinked. Or maybe he blinked and murmured. "Where am I? What happened?" he said, woozy.

"You fainted at the sight of Bernard's baby rabbits," Maureen Houdini sighed loudly as everyone piled out of the helicopter. "In other words, never fly a helicopter again, Clive."

"Come on," said Monty, now standing in front of Mr Portobello's metal fence and beckoning the others to follow. "We have very little time, we must get Potty."

The good news was that Esmé had saved everyone from a cruel and untimely death.

193

The not-so-good news was that Mr Portobello had seen the whole thing from his living room window giving him plenty of time to run downstairs and deploy his security system.

Mr Portobello had asked Keith Chalk several weeks ago to 'step up' the security at the house and had told him to fit more locks on the door and a high fence round the whole house that would add maximum protection.

While Mr Portobello knew that Esmé and Monty would not have forgotten about Potty entirely, he had not predicted that there would be a helicopter and a team of international magicians arriving any moment. Mr Portobello secured all the windows, bolted the front door, then went into the kitchen to make a nice cup of tea.

The magicians, Esmé and Monty stood in a line, contemplating the high wall in front of them.

"Oh, heavens," said Deidre. "This is a fortress, not a house."

Maureen Houdini walked up to the fence to check how sturdy it was.

"Stupeedo," she turned and called. "This is a job for you. If you could fly over the fence, then perhaps find us a way in from the inside…?"

"Great!" said Stupeedo with much excitement. "I've been waiting for this bit. I've got my special trainers on."

"And what is so special about them?" asked Maureen.

"Aha! It's all down to the Lithuanian touch paper on the heel," said Stupeedo. "I will take off with such force that I will fly like an eagle through the air, forming a perfect fifty degree arc, then I shall make my descent swiftly and – with the g-force reaching perhaps mach 3 or even double-mach 95.2 – glide straight over the fence."

"Ooh," gasped Monty.

"Ready, and…" said Stupeedo as he ransacked a trouser pocket in order to find his matches, and lit the heels of his shoes. In a flash he was in mid-air, a human bullet with his palms pressed together.

"Go, Stupeedo!" yelled Deidre.

"You can do it!" added Monty.

For one glorious moment the Great Stupeedo soared through the air like a bird, mighty and true, until he went *splat* – straight into the fence.

"Oh," he muttered as he realised he hadn't quite completed the journey. "Well, I made a hole at least."

Esmé and Monty ran up to the fence to see if Stupeedo was all right.

Esmé looked closely at the dent he had made. "This fence isn't metal, it's plastic," she said, then she noticed Stupeedo's shoes. "Your heels are still alight, by the way."

"That's it!" Stupeedo had had a brainwave. "Plastic! It's perfect."

Stupeedo took off his left shoe and started to melt the plastic around the hole in the fence, which quickly got bigger, the edges curling in on themselves like a strange synthetic flower. Soon the gap in the fence was big enough for the visitors to squeeze through.

The magicians and the Pepper twins emerged the other side, victorious.

"We're in!" said Deidre.

Mr Portobello watched from the kitchen window. "Damn those magicians," he said. "If they can make it through my fence, they're bound to make it into the house eventually. Well, no matter. Time for Plan C..." And Mr Portobello chuckled – a deep, dark chuckle.

"This house looks as if it has been built upside down," said Stupeedo, walking up to the building. He tried the front door. "It's no use. It's locked."

"Shhh!" whispered Maureen. "Mr Portobello mustn't know we're here. Using my legendary escapologist skills, I'll prise open a window and open the front door from the other side…"

"Maybe I could go round the back and see if there's another way in before Mr Portobello realises we're here?" suggested Esmé.

"Too late," came a voice.

The magicians and the Pepper twins turned to see the figure of Mr Portobello, a towelling bathrobe covering his ill-fitting suit, at the front door. "What are you doing here at this time of night? You've just woken me up. I'll call the police."

"I don't think you will," Esmé replied. "Now, where's Potty?"

"I told you, he went back on the boat just after you. Why don't you come in and have a look if you don't believe me?" said Mr Portobello, yawning. "You won't find anything."

The magicians exchanged glances. Esmé and Monty led the way, stepping with trepidation and a small amount of befuddlement into Mr Portobello's home.

"Do come in, and shut the door behind you."

As they entered, they could hear light

classical music coming from the radio in the kitchen.

"You can search the house from top to bottom," shouted Mr Portobello over the noise. "Why not start in the corridor and work your way up?" he suggested. "You won't find anyone."

The magicians filed into the corridor, only to find the Giant Penny Fall blocking their way.

"Can you move this obstacle, please?" Stupeedo asked Mr Portobello.

"We want to look upstairs," said Maureen.

"Um…" replied Mr Portobello. "Just a sec…" he mumbled, fiddling with a switch on the back of the machine. "Just, er, tying my shoelace."

"But you aren't wearing any shoes…" said Esmé. "You've got slippers on."

"Look here, Mr…" said Stupeedo, taking one step forward.

With a loud spinning sound the Giant Penny Fall rattled into action, simultaneously lighting up and moving forward, millimetre by millimetre. The magicians and the Peppers twins were forced back so that they were all eventually pressed up against the front door. Maureen Houdini began to try and pick the lock, but Esmé could see it was stuck. Team Potty was trapped.

The pennies contained within the glass cabinet shone bright as stars while sharp metallic levers pushed them onward and outward, but never to fall. With a smooth

203

shrank noise an oversize pincer lifted high over the cabinet and dropped the teddy bear over Maureen, who managed to catch it.

"Mr Portobello!" shouted Maureen crossly, clutching the nylon bear. "Stop this machine at once."

Mr Portobello simply smiled and said nothing as the machine continued to move towards the visitors. The pincer began to snap at the group, then hovered over Monty in particular and snapped some more. Music still drifted in from the kitchen – a cloying violin solo.

"Argh!" cried Monty, trying to back away but finding that he was already against the wall. "Get it away from me."

Maureen threw the teddy bear over the

machine at Mr Portobello but she missed –
and anyway, it was little use as a weapon.

Snap, snap! went the pincer.

"Just tell us where Potty is!" yelled Esmé.

Mr Portobello pressed another button on
the Giant Penny Fall and the pincer opened
its jaws wide, moving in to ensnare the Pepper
twins and the magicians in its evil grip.

Deidre struggled to get free – Clive and
Stupeedo too – but the pincer's grip got
tighter with every move they made. Monty
and Esmé tried to break free by wriggling
but the pincer would not give way.

Maureen, however, was in her element. As
daughter of the famous Barry Houdini she
knew that now was not the time to disappoint
her father's legacy and duly started to fish in

205

her front pockets for her pliers in order to attack the pincer. She would not be foiled by a simple arcade machine. She had escaped from perilous circumstances ten times worse: under the ocean, next to a bag of snakes, on top of a moving bus...

However, as soon as Maureen had wiggled the pliers from her left to right hand, Mr Portobello snatched them.

"You don't get out of here that easily," he told her, laughing as he walked away, and leaving Esmé, Monty and the International Magic Guys in a bit of a pickle – a rather large pickle. In fact, maybe the biggest pickle that any of them had been in for a long, long while.

An excerpt from

Dr Pompkins – Totality Magic

TRICK: How to Force a Card

During a trick, you may sometimes need to *make* someone choose the card you want them to, without them realising it. This is called 'forcing a card'. One way to do it is like so:

Place the card you want chosen on top of the pack, ask someone to cut the pack and place the lower half (A) at right angles across the upper half (B) in order to mark the cut.

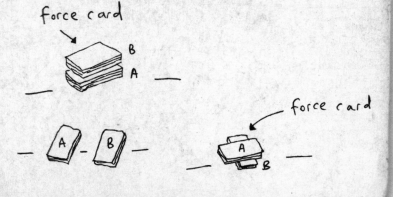

Now you must chat for a few moments – wildly and as full-throatily as possible – so that your audience member forgets which half is which. Maybe talk about oranges or the state of the Euro.

Then ask your pal to lift off the top pack (A) and look at the top card of the lower pack (B).

As this was the original top card of the pack you have done it, *mon brave*.

Ego

To be a magician you must be confident, smart and well-rehearsed. However, you must not be too full of yourself. A big ego is easy to spot and hard to like. A big ego is *never* something to cultivate. The world of magic is a wonderful place but it is about *sharing* magic, not just performing it and savouring the applause. The art of magic relies on the wonders of perception, expectation and belief. There is no room for superiority. You must humble yourself at all times. "The good magician travels third class," as the great Ali Bongo once said.

In all totality,

Dr Pompkins

CHAPTER THIRTEEN

High-visibility Jet Pack

"Should we read the tea leaves?" Tabitha asked her sister as they waited impatiently for news.

"No, if there's something I need to know, I'll hear it on the wind…" said Twinkle. "If I listen carefully, the spirits will definitely whisper something."

Tabitha waited as Twinkle wrinkled her nose and closed her eyes. "Anything?" she asked Twinkle.

"All I can hear is light classical music."

"And no key words or visions?"

"Not this time," replied Twinkle. "What do you think that means?"

"I'm hoping it's a good sign."

The Table sisters had armed themselves with woolly blankets to keep out the cold and were both spying on the moonlit Crab Pie Island through binoculars from the roof of the Sea Spray Theatre. Tabitha and Twinkle had seen the helicopter land and the magicians enter, but after half an hour had gone by there was no more activity. Tabitha and Twinkle feared the worst – and of course the worst was true – that Mr Portobello had kidnapped them *all*.

"What do we do now?" Tabitha asked Twinkle.

"I just don't know," sighed Twinkle. "This rescue operation is not really going to plan, is it?"

A yawning Keith joined them on the roof.

"Seen anything?" he asked Twinkle. "It's getting late."

"Not a peep. What if they never return?" said Twinkle with tears in her eyes.

"Right, I've had enough," Keith said suddenly. "If anyone's got to help, it's Keith Chalk. I know Mr Portobello, I know the house. I'm going to rescue the Peppers, Potty and the International Magic Guys – and, you know, I think I've got the right gadget to do it!"

Keith ran back downstairs into the theatre, then reappeared on the roof again a few minutes later holding a high-visibility vest.

"Ta-da!" he said, displaying the type of garment that someone mending a road surface would wear.

"Are you going cycling?" asked Tabitha.

"We certainly won't lose you in that," said Twinkle. "But I don't quite see…"

"It's a turbo jet pack. There are rocket boosters sewn in the back and it has padded shoulders, in case of any accidents. It's visible in cloud, fog, snow and rain. It's waterproof, fireproof, child-friendly and ecological."

Tabitha and Twinkle were visibly impressed. High-visibility impressed.

"How remarkable!" said Tabitha. "It's the

vest that does *everything*. The fabric is so reflective, the boosters look so powerful…"

"What does this breast pocket hold?" asked Twinkle.

"It contains satellite navigation, a smartphone that links on to the battery pack, three different flavours of high-energy nutty bars, a Swiss army knife and a torch," Keith explained.

"And now I will launch myself from this roof and rescue our friends from the clutches of Mr Portobello," he continued, moving to the edge. "Wish me luck!" He beamed with anticipation. "I've just got to find the right button…

"One, two, three…" The jacket gave a fizzling sound then suddenly Keith was

214

launched into the sky, like an even higher-visibility-than-usual firework.

"*Ooooooh…*" remarked Tabitha.

"*Aaaaah…*" said Twinkle.

"He looks just like Superman," cooed Tabitha.

Keith Chalk shot through the amber heavens with grace and style. It was his first full flight in the jacket, as he'd just been working on blueprints and computer simulations until now.

Brrrring brrrring!

It was at this moment Keith heard a ringing coming from his breast pocket. His smartphone! He had forgotten to turn it off.

Brrrring brrrring! it continued to ring from

his pocket. Who was calling at such a late hour?

The problem was, Keith thought as he sailed through the chilly air at forty miles per hour, the phone was linked to – and now draining the – energy supply. Keith had only accounted for energy use in flight mode – without considering the additional use of superfluous gadgets. Unfortunately, therefore, Keith fell from the skies at an alarming rate and dipped quickly and coolly into the ocean.

"Bother," he cursed, as he thrashed about in the water.

On the theatre roof the Table sisters had wasted no time in picking up their trusty binoculars and watching Keith's heroic journey through the sky. They looked on as he crashed into now the red sea, reflecting the sunset on the horizon.

"Oh, deary me," gasped Twinkle.

"Oh, deary, deary me," said Tabitha. "Another one down."

While his visitors were still trapped in the grips of a giant pincer, Mr Portobello had had an idea. He went upstairs to the living room to ring Keith on his mobile, wondering if he could find out whether the Giant Penny Fall did anything else – other than grip things in its nasty metal claws. Keith's phone rang and rang but there was no reply. Mr Portobello didn't know what to do next, so he turned on the television and settled down for a quiet

217

evening in front of the (large) telly to watch a favourite show of his, *Badger Festival.*

Back downstairs, the magicians were getting restless.

"Do you think we'll get out alive?" whispered a nervous Stupeedo.

"Of course we will, we're magicians. It's our job," replied Maureen, trying to sound assured.

"I hope Bernard and her babies are OK," wondered Deidre aloud. "I have an awful feeling that I left the helicopter door open…"

"What's the worst that can happen?" asked Stupeedo. "They'll do a bit of snuffling, eat some grass, look cute."

"I suppose so," answered Deidre.

"It's not the rabbits that we need to worry about," said Maureen. "It's how on earth we're going to get out of here… The front door is definitely jammed."

Outside the house, Bernard and her babies *had* escaped the helicopter and were indeed snuffling. They must have smelt from afar the chewed stubs of Mr Portobello's Chantenay carrots outside the kitchen window as, having crawled through the hole in the fence, that is where they were headed. Unfortunately for Mr Portobello, the carrot detritus had been thrown next to some electric cables, part of the primitive energy supply that served the island home. The rabbits found the

carrots and started munching. And with one light crunch, Bernard accidentally chewed through the main electricity supply between the generator and the house. Bernard felt a tingle of warm electricity run through her furry body, but apart from that she was unscathed.

Woophmm!

"Hey! Who turned out all the lights?" murmured Stupeedo. Then: "Maureen, stop wiggling."

"The Giant Penny Fall has just turned itself off!" whispered Maureen Houdini. "The pincer has loosened its grip! We're free!"

The magicians and the Pepper twins eagerly disentangled themselves from the

giant pincer and Stupeedo gave everyone a high five.

"Right, you two," whispered Maureen to the twins. "Let's creep upstairs and find out where Mr Portobello's put Potty."

Esmé and Monty both nodded silently.

"If Mr Portobello hears anything," Maureen continued, "then at least someone can distract him while the other two run upstairs to warn us. Deidre, Stupeedo, Clive – you stand guard here at the foot of the stairs."

Esmé, Monty and Maureen crept upstairs most carefully and most silently. They passed Mr Portobello who was far too busy meddling with leads – trying to work out why there was no power – to notice them.

There was nothing on the third floor but on the fourth the twins and Maureen were greeted by a large door – and a small broom cupboard.

"Let's try the door," whispered Esmé. "Is it locked?"

Monty gently tried the handle. "Yes, it won't open," he said.

"Uncle Potty!" he whispered through the door frame, but there was no reply.

Monty turned to Maureen. "Can you pick the lock?"

"No problem," replied Maureen. She fished out a pair of tweezers, a hairpin and a trunk key from her trouser pocket.

Now they could hear shuffling coming from behind the door.

"It's OK," Monty whispered. "We won't be long."

Maureen skilfully undid the lock with the tweezers in a matter of seconds and the door opened wide to reveal a darkened room, lit only by a small candle at the far end where a table and two chairs stood.

Potty was sitting by the table with four glass bottles in front of him. He turned towards the door.

"Esmé, Monty – and Maureen Houdini herself!" he beamed, standing up. "You have found me!"

The Pepper twins rushed over to hug Potty.

"I'm so glad you're OK," said Esmé, giving him a squeeze.

"Have you been up here all this time?" asked Monty, looking up at Uncle Potty and thinking that he somehow looked taller.

"Yes, yes, but it was not too unpleasant," replied Potty. "Now, let me introduce you to a friend of... Where are you, Gary?"

A dusty head appeared from underneath the table.

"If we could just make a hole in the end of the bottle... then the frog can... Oh!" Gary Meringue's bearded face smiled broadly. "Are we... *Surely not...* Are we saved?"

"I think so," said Esmé.

"I'm Gary Meringue," said the bearded magician, holding out his hand. "Delighted to meet you! I've been here ages." Esmé noticed there were long strands of dust

hanging from his jacket sleeves like willow leaves.

"This is Esmé and Monty – my niece and nephew," explained Potty.

"Ooh, I've heard so much about you," said Gary who, under all that dust, wore a bow tie and a suit. "All good things."

"And this is Maureen Houdini, daughter of the late, great Barry Houdini." Potty pointed to Maureen, who was still standing by the doorway.

"I am honoured to meet you," said Gary Meringue, bowing towards Maureen – who smiled in return.

"Now, what's stopping us?" asked Potty. "Let's get straight back to the theatre to work on the show."

"We've just got to deal with Mr Portobello first," Esmé replied, giving Potty one more hug. "Let him know that his dreadful plan is over."

They all nodded at each other, and then Esmé took the lead as the five captives crept quietly down the stairs to the kitchen below.

An excerpt from

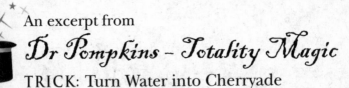

Dr Pompkins – Totality Magic

TRICK: Turn Water into Cherryade

Wedge a paper cup inside a large jug using a bath sponge or anything that is absorbent.

Fill the paper cup with cherryade or a similarly bright-coloured drink and announce that you have special powers and – *za zing!* – you will turn water into cherryade!

Take a glass of water and pour it into the sponge part of the jug, which will soak up the water.

Waggle your hands over the jug and shout, 'To the Pompkins!' (maybe) then pour the jug – the cherryade in the cup will flow into the glass.

Not that anybody should be drinking litres of fizzy pop these days, on account of future teeth and gum health problems. I prefer brandy.

cherryade

Stamina

While we have made much of practice and the art of a good stage performance, we have not mentioned stamina. To be a magician you must be able to concentrate over the course of two or three tricks at first, and to do this you need to make sure you are prepared. A good night's sleep, a breakfast of fruits and grains and a real *mental focus* will be your aids for this. The more you perform an array of different tricks, the more the mind will be able to 'lock into' the task and the fewer mistakes will be made. Your mind is a muscle, train it well. And do not watch too much television or pop videos.

In all totality,

Dr Pompkins

CHAPTER FOURTEEN

Another Flying Machine

Hearing muffled footsteps walking down the stairs and into the kitchen Mr Portobello put two and two together – Gary Meringue and the Potty Magician had escaped. Mr Portobello, the local businessman and sort-of executive, knew that he was in big trouble. Having no more resources – no Plan D or Plan E – Mr Portobello did the only thing any executive businessman could do in his position: he decided to escape.

Mr Portobello was not a natural inventor but he had watched Keith on and off and felt that he knew the basics. As a result, in the last three weeks he had done something he was immensely proud of – he had secretly built a flying machine and harboured it in the broom cupboard at the top of the house. Now was the time to use it. Of course, the machine was rudimentary, but Mr Portobello had faith that this was the vehicle to get him out of this sticky situation. He could jet to the train station in town and get a ticket to the capital. From there he would fly to somewhere hot like Spain.

Mr Portobello ran upstairs to the top floor and opened the cupboard door. There it was – a magnificent creature, made from tin foil, balsa wood, Blu-tack and assorted nuts and screws – covered with a fine bubble-wrap mesh, constructed from polystyrene webbing, the sort that apples are commonly packed in.

"My beauty!" cried Mr Portobello, who had based his creation on the sketches of Leonardo Da Vinci's flying machine. "You will take me out of here!" He had visions of himself as a god of some sort, soaring over the rooftops of people who were poorer and therefore had far fewer chrome fittings and bendy taps than he did.

Mr Portobello strapped himself into the flying machine. He felt fantastic. The wings were weightless, the wooden structure firm but light. Mr Portobello felt all-powerful –

everything was in its place. *I rule the world!* he thought.

This was all very fine, but just as Mr Portobello was about to take off on the voyage of a lifetime, he realised there was one problem. In order to catch the breeze he would have to leave from this, the top floor. And yet when he looked at the prison-like windows that he had specifically asked to be installed, he knew he'd never get himself and the flying machine out in one piece. The spaces between the bars were too small. If he ran downstairs and tried to take off from the shore he would not get any sort of lift off. What was he to do?

With a leaden heart and wounded pride, Mr Portobello released himself from the winged wonder. He sighed. He would simply have to run downstairs and swim to the shore. Then walk to the train station, go to the capital, get on the plane, etc.

Mr Portobello thundered down the stairs, through the corridor, out of the front door and through the gap in the fence. Potty, the IMG magicians and the Pepper twins looked on, stunned.

"Come back!" shouted Maureen. "We want to arrest you for kidnapping."

Within half a minute everyone had scrambled outside and watched as Mr Portobello threw his shoes and jacket in the air. He raced to the shoreline, dived into the cold water and started to swim in the direction of the mainland.

Monty turned to Esmé. "What on earth is he doing?"

"I have absolutely no idea," Esmé replied. "The water is not particularly inviting at this time of night."

Mr Portobello continued to splash about, but it was clear that he was not a strong swimmer. Maureen squinted at the sea ahead.

"It looks like…" she said. "I don't believe it. There's *two* of them."

While Mr Portobello's head was bobbing in the water in one spot, another head was also bobbing nearby.

"That looks like Keith Chalk in a high-visibility vest!" cried Esmé. "You're right, Maureen. Two men overboard!"

Esmé ran to the helicopter and grabbed the well-worn manual. Flicking through, she saw that there was a rescue rope attached to every vehicle 'as standard'. If she could fly the helicopter again they could save Keith and catch Mr Portobello in one fell swoop.

"It's time to make a sea rescue. A double sea rescue," said Esmé, purposefully.

"Really?" asked Clive, who had not really enjoyed the last journey.

"Yes," said Esmé. "Although you are allowed to sit in the back and close your eyes for as long as you need to."

The magicians and the Pepper twins boarded the helicopter. Deidre sat in the back with Bernard, the baby rabbits and Clive.

Quickly and more smoothly this time, Esmé managed to lift the helicopter up. There was plenty of help from her technicians, Monty and Maureen, who kept their eyes glued to the manual and supported her all the way. The levers seemed easier to control this time and the helicopter started to glide through the sky.

Shortly, they were hovering directly above Mr Portobello and Keith, both splashing not-very-usefully in the sea, losing energy and fight with every stroke.

Monty had found the 'emergency megaphone' (fitted on every *EeezyHover HC2100* as standard too) under his seat, rolled down the window and was barking at the two failing swimmers below.

"It's OK, you two," he said. "We'll have you up in a minute. *Roger.*"

Maureen found the button that let the hook descend.

"Just grab on to the hook when it gets to you," instructed Monty. "Hold on tight, please. *Over and out.*"

The hook descended on the long, thick rope and soon Keith had managed to take hold of it. The rope had been coated, he noticed in a fix-it man sort of way, in a very interesting, non-slip rubber resin. It took Mr Portobello a few more attempts to grab the hook, but finally he did so too.

"All OK to travel?" asked Monty through the megaphone.

And so, as dawn approached, the

helicopter made its way – with the two bedraggled figures swaying below it – over the short distance to Crab Pie Pier.

"Ooh, this is smashing, isn't it?" Twinkle said to her sister as they viewed the events unfolding at sea. "A thrilling ocean adventure."

"Come on, Esmé and Monty, that's the way!" shouted Tabitha, jumping up and down as much as her knees would let her.

The sun was rising, colouring the sky a warm red. Jimi stood alongside the Table sisters with two large trays of food – and an armful of towels for Keith and Mr Portobello, who looked rather wet.

"Is that Esmé at the controls?" Jimi asked, craning his neck to see.

"Looks like it," responded Tabitha.

"My, she's doing incredibly well with what is a difficult and precise machine," Jimi noted.

"Hi, Jimi! All right down there, *Roger*?" Monty was still bellowing through the megaphone. "I'm just going to drop these two off on the walkway," he shouted. "If you all can make sure Mr Portobello doesn't escape, then we'll land on the tattoo parlour. Over and out."

"Over and out!" called Twinkle.

The helicopter hovered over the walkway, and Keith and Mr Portobello landed in a heap on the pier, Jimi and the Table sisters running down to meet them. An extremely damp Keith slowly got up and Jimi handed him a towel. Twinkle and Tabitha walked up to an equally sodden Mr Portobello, both sisters with hands on hips.

"You're going nowhere, sunshine," said Tabitha.

Mr Portobello's lower lip quivered.

"Now, come on, Tabs," he said. "Have a heart... *Twinks?*"

The sisters looked at each other, and Tabitha gave her sister the 'thumbs up'. They both counted to three then Tabitha dealt Mr Portobello a firm blow to the knees and he toppled over. Twinkle seized the moment and sat on him. Tabitha joined her.

"You're a criminal, Mr Portobello," announced Tabitha. "We gave you enough chances. Now we're going to call the police."

Twinkle closed her eyes and wrinkled her nose.

"Twinkle Table," said Tabitha, "we can't call them through the spirit world. They don't operate like that. Jimi, would you…?"

Jimi Sinha turned to Tabitha. "Certainly, madam," he said, finding his mobile phone. "It would be my pleasure."

Mr Portobello started to growl.

"It's no use you grumbling now, Mr Portobello," said Twinkle. "You've made your bed, you're going to lie in it."

"I predict tough times ahead for you, Mr Portobello," said Twinkle, arms crossed. "But I foresee that justice will be done."

An excerpt from

Dr Pompkins – Totality Magic

TRICK: Pop Goes the Lollipop

To prepare, fix a small cellophane-wrapped lollipop securely to one end of a forty-centimetre piece of elastic.

Pin the other end up your sleeve.

When you perform, show the audience the lollipop out of your sleeve and hold it so that the elastic is hidden behind your wrist {see fig. 1}. Now pretend to drop the lolly into a paper bag while really letting the elastic pull it back up your sleeve.

Now blow up the paper bag and burst it – in all totality, the lollipop has vanished.

———

Simply *brillia-rilliant.*

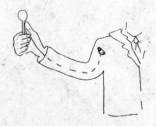

Thank You...

...for your company on this long, silky journey through the magic hintersphere. There are many things to learn still, many classics that we can find inspiration from. Keep learning – read magic, observe magic and practise magic. This crazy trip of ours may, indeed, never end, but I love it so and I hope you do too.

In all totality,

Dr Pompkins

CHAPTER FIFTEEN

A Bright Future

Potty's show was only a day away. Although everyone was exhausted from yesterday's events they knew that they had to do their utmost to make the performance as incredible as it possibly could be.

Inside the theatre, Potty and Keith started to get the props ready, calling over to each other, giving directions – becoming more and more exhilarated by the sheer ambition of the show itself.

However, despite the excitement of recent events and witnessing the glorious rescue from Mr Portobello's island from a good vantage point, the Table sisters' mood was rather glum.

Tabitha was first to pinpoint the problem. "It's wonderful that Mr Portobello is in jail," she explained. "But now we have no one to buy the theatre, not even anyone to make a *low* offer."

Twinkle sadly agreed. "I guess we'll have to live in that poky little caravan all our lives."

"Ahem." A figure appeared in the main doorway. "I heard that there was a friend of mine in town and I happened to be passing by…"

The sharply-dressed, pointy-toed Nigella

Spoon walked into the Sea Spray and put her shiny handbag down on one of the seats towards the back. Nigella was head of the Pan-Continental Magic Corporation. She oversaw hundreds of magic clubs including the International Magic Guys, which, after their show-stopping performance last summer, was now one of her favourite associations. Nigella smiled broadly (something that she had been practising recently) and strode up to Uncle Potty.

"Hello, Potty!" she said, shaking him by the hand. Her tone was naturally formal but it could not hide the real warmth that she felt for the Potty Magician. "I couldn't resist coming from New York City. The first show is tomorrow, am I right?"

"Nigella!" exclaimed Potty. "I am chuffed to bits that you have made such a long journey."

"My, this is a beautiful old theatre!" Nigella remarked, looking around. "Who owns it?"

After much talk, Nigella was made aware of the Table sisters' situation.

"I'm always interested in new locations," she said.

"The Sea Spray is going to become the coast's top magic venue," boasted Monty. "Potty's playing for a fortnight, and now we've scheduled Gary Meringue to follow. After that, Clive Pastel."

"And we've found an amazing technical genius in Keith Chalk," added Esmé. "He can make every show a million times better.

He knows how to build absolutely *anything*."

"In all totality," Potty finished.

"Hm," pondered Nigella. "What sort of price are you looking for?"

Tabitha and Nigella conferred in private for a moment, then broke away as Nigella took out a notebook and pencil from her skirt pocket and jotted something down.

Potty's fluffy eyebrow rose higher than it had in a long time. Maureen and Deidre craned to hear Nigella's verdict. The Table sisters waited, mouths agape, salivating slightly.

"I'll take it – I'll buy the Sea Spray Theatre," announced Nigella looking up from her notebook. "I think it has great potential."

"That's wonderful!" said Twinkle. "Now, I

just have to contact the spirits and let them know..." Twinkle closed her eyes, held out her arms and started humming.

"That's very good of you, Miss Spoon," said Tabitha, who shook Nigella's hand over and over again. "The Sea Spray won't let you down."

The delicious aroma of Jimi's snacks was by now filling the air – and the delicious aroma of a Bright Future joined in too. The smell of success was not far away either.

"This is wonderful news," exclaimed Potty. "Now, good people, we must get on. We have a show to rehearse!"

"Can Bernard get involved?" asked Deidre.

"Any use for a human cannonball?" enquired the Great Stupeedo and, at once,

the great rolling magic show began to take shape.

"… and an escapologist?" asked Maureen.

"Anyone want another Thai summer roll?" said Jimi.

Esmé watched proudly as they all found a role to play in Potty's performance. Even Gary Meringue wanted to join in.

The next day, new posters lined Crab Pie Pier. An 'extended run' at the Sea Spray Theatre for Potty, with a big billing for 'fabulous magical inventor Keith Chalk'. Next to it was a poster that read '£10 for a future you'll never forget!' with a picture of the smiling Table sisters against the backdrop of a charming new bungalow cottage on Tide Street.

Afterword by Dr Pompkins

As I recover from major leg surgery following a particularly hairy trick involving a circular saw in the warm climes of northern Budapest, I hope that you will have learned much from my tips and advice. I would ask you to go out straight away, into your new dawn, and practise what you have been taught. There is no time like the present; if there is magic to be done, the early bird catches the worm. And then hides it in a specially concealed trouser pocket.

Adieu,

Dr Pompkins

Coming Soon...

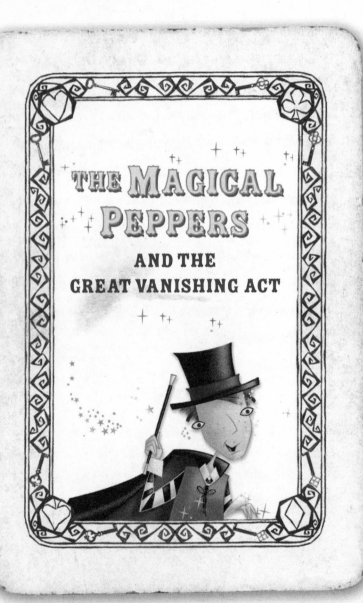

THE MAGICAL PEPPERS

**AND THE
GREAT VANISHING ACT**